Oona

Oona

ALICE LYONS

THE LILLIPUT PRESS
DUBLIN

First published 2020 by
THE LILLIPUT PRESS
62–63 Sitric Road, Arbour Hill
Dublin 7, Ireland
www.lilliputpress.ie

Paperback ISBN 9781843517719

This is a work of fiction. All characters, organizations and events portrayed in
this novel are either products of the author's imagination or are used fictitiously.

Arrowhead drawings by Hazel Walker courtesy Paul Kane Gallery, Dublin.
Arrowhead drawings are from artefacts collected in Paterson, New Jersey, in
the 1940s.
Cover photo by Alice Lyons. Inside flaps: *Saint Bernadino Resuscitating a
Drowned Child* by Sano di Pietro. c.1450 from Christiansen, Keith, Laurence
B. Kanter, and Carl Brandon Strehlke, *Painting in Renaissance Siena, 1420–1500*
(New York 1988); private collection.
Excerpt(s) from I HAD TROUBLE IN GETTING TO SOLLA SOLLEW
by Dr. Seuss © Dr. Seuss Enterprises, L.P. 1965, renewed 1993. Used by
permission of Random House Children's Books, a division of Penguin
Random House LLC.
Graves, Robert, 'Flying Crooked', in *Collected Poems* (London 2000). Poem
reprinted with permission of the estate of Robert Graves and Carcanet Press.

A CIP record for this title is available from The British Library.

10 9 8 7 6 5 4 3 2 1

The Lilliput Press gratefully acknowledges the financial support of the
Arts Council/An Chomhairle Ealaíon.

Set in 11pt on 15.8pt Jensen by Marsha Swan
Printed in Poland by Drukarnia Skelniarz

Mirror is going really badly. Nobody has any idea of what it's about. All hopeless. Sizov saw it in order to decide the question of the two parts, and he had no idea what it was about either. The material keeps falling apart, it doesn't make a whole. Altogether it is all hopeless.

—Andrei Tarkovsky, diary entry,
17 March 1974, Moscow.

Your soul is just a length of baby.

—Fanny Howe

Oona (key)

4 THE MAW

5 SHITE

6 CLASHYBEG

7 GALILEELEELEELEELEELEELEELEELEELEELEELEELY

I

SANCTUM

I

I have diminished myself relentlessly.
    Why?
Because these fragments –

    because I am in pieces.

When I was a baby, she said, *Oona, say WATER. WA-TER.*
I held her gaze, set my teeth, parted my lips. Then sent air and spittle
between my teeth: *TSISST TSISST.*
Bubbles tickled my lips.

Unh. Unh was her reply.
Oona, say WA-TER. WA-TER.

I'm saying it!, I felt/said in-baby-side.
TSISST (bubbles) *TSISST* (bubbles). Syllables I said emphatically
and with her WA-TER rhythm.

This made her laugh. I made her laugh.

3

Maybe
 she didn't get the time.
 she figured telling me equalled death.
 she decided that silence was life.
 she knew I knew and figured that was plenty.
 she hadn't the right terms.
 she said *terminal cancer* and I didn't hear.
 she didn't think I'd mind.
 she prayed a miracle'd change everything.
 she was afraid it'd kill me.
 she was afraid it'd kill her.
 she didn't want heartbreak.
 she didn't want my heartbreak.
 she figured if she kept the truth in, the truth mightn't be true.
 she'd rather live with the lie than die with the truth.
 she didn't think.
 she was thinking but I didn't figure in her thinking.
 she'd rather die than tell me she was dying as that meant it
  was true.
 she figured she'd let me fill in the blanks.
 she kept telling herself she'd tell me the next day.
She died the next day.

4

We lived in a family.
A dad. Her, me.
Her laughing. Me making her laugh. Me making her tea.
Her reading me the *Arabian Nights* my head in her lap.
Dim lamplight.
Blue TV sheen in the middle distance.
Her bright mind, sharp and fierce.
Her mind a star that fell in a blue lake.
Way she pursed her lips when she deep-smiled, eye edges creasing.
Braid between us unbreakable at the chest area.
Yes, the heart.

Ireland is an island.
Arrived age nine and Ireland invaded.

Green green green talk talk talk grey sky grey sky grey sky – very near – hedge hedge wall wall bull sheep sheep sheep ass ass wall wall wall cart cart cart sheep sheep sheep calf sheep calf calf bull bull bull wall turf fire turf fire turf fire turf fire.

Acrid turf burn scent breath printed in me.
Relatives chatted
flagrantly.
Claimed as family by them.
Great Aunt Margaret in a hairnet and slubby cardigan.

UncleAuntMargaretNualaBernadineGerardineMarianPatricia-
FrancesIda.
They hadn't much.
Cattle, an ass, turf in the barn.
Wet farm.
Me in my pressed white shirt making the limewash walls seem blue-grey.
Yes, I am a Yank with my trimmed hair and well-laundered dresses.
I wasn't an I.
My edges blurred.
Ireland filled me up in the places I wasn't.

Big suburb gaps in me.
Mist, which they call *misht*.
Uncle Ant cut peat and gave me a piece.
I wrapped it in newspaper and stuck it in my blue Pan Am bag.
Desire.
It was in the way way back in my walnut cabinet.
A teenage Tuesday I hunkered in, grabbed it
then stuffed it further, deeper in the dark.

6

I I I I I I I I I I I I I I I I I I I I I I I I I I I I I I I I I I I I I I I I I I I I I I I I I I
I I I I I I I I I I I I I I I I I I I I I I I I I I I I I I

All my I's islanded.

A track.

My running self-stitch, repairing.

The Islands can't link up.

There is a missing thing which I must write.

Find.

In time.

I I I I I I I I I II I I I I I III I II I I I I II I I I I IIII I I I I I I I I I I
II I I I I I I II I II II III IIIIII II III II II II II II II IIIIIII II I I I
I I II II I II II II II II III I II II II I I II I I I II I

7

I remember seeing it in a display case in Venice, with Her. It was the Big France-Germany-Switzerland-Italy-Austria-Netherlands-England-Ireland American Express Bus Trip a few years after the Big Ireland Trip. I was twelve. The chastity belt in decaying leather and crude metal with a fist-sized ring. Sharp spikes went in at the centre like a reverse sea urchin. The belt guarded the lady's labia and vagina, preventing entry. If the man put his bare dick in that thing, he'd be cut bad. If she sat, the spikes'd dig in. She'd be sliced up and infected and there'd be sepsis and death.

This was in the sixteenth century.

As I grew up, I created my special chastity belt.

It was invisible but palpable, cinching seed-me.

Seed-me was dark and deep and if I gazed in, I'd get dizzy.

Spin and fall. Get eaten up.

Desire was in there, a bit decrepit already.

Let me explain.

Try.

8

EXPLAIN.
Term that frikens me.

9

Papier-mâché was the chief material. I mixed white wheatmeal and water – made a paste. Blew up a rubber sac with air and wrapped it with wet newspaper strips. Brushed it with the wheat paste and put the thing by the fireplace. When it was dried, I stuck a needle in and burst the rubber sac. Then I had a vacant white sphere, a little bumpy, but serviceable.

The kitchen table was my science lab that weekend: it was newspaper-strewn, paint in jelly jars with brushes stuck in, papier-mâché dust, public-library texts, lined paper with handwritten scrawls, weird little diagrams. I sawed the sphere in half with her serrated knife taking care that the edges weren't jagged. I painted a half-sphere's curve with a black pupil, a blue iris and multiple spidery red veins that curved with the sphere's curve and bumped a little where the papier-mâché was uneven. The Eyeball.

In the remaining half-sphere's cave, I built the retina, the receiving place, the sanctum. My intent was making real the device that seemed the Everything Instrument in my as yet brief life. If science permitted dissecting myself I might find my place within the field. The science field.

I liked fields. Mulligan's field was the place where we played best, where Li-my-friend and I had met picking daisies when we were three. That was the myth we created. We. In the field. Where we were. Where I was. Was I there? Where was I? I was in the eye I felt. Even if I didn't feel very real, yet my eye was.

In my best Palmer penmanship, I scrivened *IRIS*, *PUPIL*, *RETINA*, *SCLERA* and defined them, taped the index cards beside the papier-mâché replicas.

The science assignment was due Tuesday.

There was the day that she

I'd been in classes all day. Dad was at the plant. A regular day
with her in her bed and nurses at her side and us absent. But it
was a different day because last night the nurses had called me
in. By her bedside. Her eyes. Where she wasn't. They were just
whites, the irises disappeared back in her head. Skin like vellum,
lips parched, rimed in white crust. Clearly she was busy dying.
They'd never said *cancer*. They'd never said *terminal*. They'd said
tummy bug, thus the drip and the meals she lacked.

This night, the nurse said, *Say night night.*

I didn't say night night. I said *Bye*.

That I held her in my yes heart.

She said, *Pray.*

I didn't pray. Didn't get what praying was.

I left, went in bed, muffled my cries in my mattress. Wet it
with my tears. Next day, I left the bus and walked Mulligan's field
as I always did at three-ish. There were pine trees between me
and the cul-de-sac where we lived. I heard Mrs Dagger's Cadillac
(Ruby Red) start up nearby. Big rumble and I knew.

The Cadillac engine ignited the truth.

The Cadillac engine busted up the lies.

This I knew, just knew:

She died while I was in freshman classes and Dad at the plant.
Nurses with her.

Mrs Dagger was intercepting me. Li-my-friend was her daughter. Mrs Dagger had been called by my father because she had died and I wasn't permitted see.

A child can't see death in this suburb we lived in.

Cadillac between me and the real – that she was dead, had been dying, that I'd been kept away.

Furtively between parted curtains in Li-my-friend's place, I watched funeral men put her in the hearse when Mrs Dagger wasn't watching. A stretcher with a stick wrapped in sheets she was. Night night. Slid in the black hearse and away.

Days later they put her in a dank dark gash in a cemetery with sterile granite placemats marking the dead there. All the names made plain. American. Sign with a red circle read: *WREATHS AND FLAGS IMPEDE GRASS CUTTING.* Wanted is this big dead lawn, easily maintained. Flat. She in there unvisited.

She never said
They never said
Then I never said.
Inside.

II

Day she died filled with textures
my feet felt everything:
ridged rubber bus steps I descended
gravel and salt – the January suburb street
Mullligan's field crabgrass and hay stubble already freezing
greasy tiles in Dagger's stale kitchen
gritty brick-edged cement steps that led up
where Dad was waiting in the hall
unfixed blue slate hall tile
way it ferried my feet a laggard inch
his camel Chesterfield flapped like an empty tent
I ran inside
cigar smell, gaberdine hand
tinkling bus change

day I ascended

Where can I dig?
In that silence.
Years, days, minutes when I didn't hear myself
my largest sea part, the part with tides.
Write that unheard language.
Where I wasn't
myself and further.

Later walked up the aisle twice thinking I knew myself when I
didn't duh.

Writing is plaiting.

A landscape, a fading language, a weird suburb.
Veer.
Plait.

My name is __na
My name is __na
My name is __na
My name is __na
My name is __na
My name is __na
My name is __na

na na na na na na na na na na na na na na na

na

na

na

na

na

na

Lamp Black deep dark clarity. Inky night-time. Titanium White chalky, assertive. Zinc White weaker, lacking tint-verve. Ultra-marine Blue can be black in a puddle until the hue leaks wild at the pinguid edges. Cerulean Blue – very much itself, unkeen re: mixing. Cerulean likes singleness. Viridian Green – middling. Terre Verte, a bit weak but it has its place. Cadmium Red, Cadmium Yeller in light, medium and deep types: nuclear hue. Raw Sienna: earthy, muddy. Burnt Sienna, in the nutmeg family while Burnt Umber is a melted Hershey Bar. Raw Umber greenish yak dung. Alizarin: thin, winey and inky. Permeates everything. Same with Prussian Blue – my least-liked pigments – the bad way they behave, bullying everything.

2

MICHANAGRAPE

I was split-level like the Panzavecchias' ranch-style place where Apache Street and Pawnee Lane met. Upstairs, in the sunlit-den me, I was nice. Read all the signals, was well-behaved. Acted as if she wasn't in bed always uneating with a drip in her arm, nurses at her bedside, busy dying. Attended cheerleading practice as usual. In a basement party with mates, I admitted she might actually be terminal – cancer I guessed, explained I hadn't seen her eat in weeks, that we had nurses all day and all night at her bedside.

Terry in the sweaty teenage basement gathering, when I'd said my bit, hissed, *Shh. Think it and it might happen!*

Her champagne terrier hair became white, wan and patchy. I knew.

Sister Eugene, a nun-relative I'd barely ever seen, was making frequent visits. I knew.

Her sudden relenting – letting me get my ears pierced at twelve rather than at sixteen, as decreed when she'd dug her heels in years back, and I had hated her strictness. I knew.

Drip in her arm. I knew.

Her in bed at Thanksgiving. I knew.

Then at Christmas. I knew I knew.

The paper scrap with her handwriting and all the names and the jewellery items they'd get. I knew I knew I knew.

In this underside split-level ranch me, I was aware. Truth leaked in unimpeded. In my basement air were sensings. Temperatures, shivers, plummets, eruptings, tightenings, releasings, halts, acidic pulses, warmings, freezings, spikes, gluts, glitches, cryptic, slight registers, trembles, gurgles. As the adults in my midst talked, walked, *were* – all these sensings happened. I registered them silently, packed them all away in my split-level ranch basement space, dragging this feeling-bag everywhere with me.

I knew I knew I knew. In the feeling-bag I knew.

I wasn't mute. It wasn't like that. I was actually cute and I talked talk a Jersey teen talked:

Pick me up at this time talk.

Bus arrives at such-and-such a time talk.

Can I buy a Perry Ellis sweater? talk.

Will Ken call? talk.

Janet Crutch is a bitch talk.

What're we having at dinner? talk.

I was slaving away at being the average teen. The things I said were unremarkable. The thing I didn't remark: HELP.

The bridge between my head talk and my belly talk was fucked up. Actually, there wasn't a bridge. Just the upstairs and basement ranch with an absent staircase. Dual levels, each having a life by itself. Chastity-belted I was in my middle. Cinched at the waist tight.

This split-level place. M-ther – missing.

Her cleaning knack: the scrubbing, shining, bleaching and refreshing ability. The saucepan-gleaming gift. The creative dinner-making, setting an abundant table each evening. Leaving appliances, sink, surfaces, tiles all twinkling. Nary a breadcrumb, nary a greasy splatter anywhere. Smithereened after she died, her gleaming kitchen had a greasy film that defied scrubbing. Rescue Pads, little lime-green rectangles, scrubby cleaning things. These were her washing-up implements. Afterwards, Rescue Pads never did the trick, didn't live up their name.

The laundry still smelled like bleach and pets. Bleaching stirring stick in the bleaching basin leaning in the laundry sink. Plaid blanket pet bed still creased in her neat way. Bench with the spindled back – she paid the antique man a pittance – standing tall in the hall. Stickley desk beside it. Upstairs, drawers stacked with her beautiful sweaters infused with her smells. Tweed suit she'd picked up in Galway. These things she selected. Just sitting there dumbly, accusing in their thingness. In their silence.

Winds blew up the stairs, in all the spaces we'd lived in. Everything shivered. If I knew she was dying upstairs in the single bed while it was happening, maybe I'd have released my attachment a little bit. As it was, it was excruciating living with things, in this place she wasn't but was. I was thirteen. Class, friends, beginner's sex, keg parties. *The best time in life*, adults had repeated. Enduring manic and depressed Dad.

In the upper ranch, I was stiff-lipped. I was present in principle. Captured by Dad's camera in Super 8 mm cheerleading films, in snaps at art fairs, my painting and drawing medals displayed at family gatherings, smiling. Well, I was spreading lips, displaying my teeth. In the under-level, sensings turbidly swirled but upstairs I was unaware. Dragged this gut-suitcase everywhere with me. It was inaccessible luggage. Like the tree with the awful malignancy in its svelteness. A gall it's called. Ink was made with it in the past. Me lugging this gall everywhere.

I read: gulag narratives, kulak sufferings, Nazi shits killing everything.
Ukrainian and Irish famine tales, Native American massacres.
The hard lives: refugees, 'asylum seekers', exiles.
The friend that had been in hiding during the Red Khmer time;

they'd killed her medic parents. I empathized and used such narratives as an escape.

My empathy was a guise, in part.

Pain is pain is pain.

I parcelled mine up, sent it away, put it in elsewheres,

scattered it everywhere thinking I might shift it,

in bad faith with myself.

Did I shatter in a flash like an incendiary device?

Did I particle-ize the minute she left us?

It happened gradually.

A hundred girls in pleated check skirts scattering: all me-pieces.

Self. Effervesced.

I chased extremities, margins, elsewheres.

Liked maps.

Ran ran ran filling that self space up with literatures, art, travels,

learning (all the degrees I accumulated), yearning.

Had a brain and creativity.

Writing, painting, drawing.

Spent years in academe's verges.

(Never in the centre; I was invisibility-dedicated.)

Teachers were always a little surprised at my well-written papers

because I didn't speak in class.

Filled up with their praise, I felt affirmed,

briefly.

Sure I knew I was missing a Thing I Needed.

What?

It was In There but inaccessible.

I kept travelling away, leaning elsewhere.

I am dying, daughter, I can't bear parting.
My life has been brief. The me that will never blaze – I grieve it.
A keen that breaks the riverbanks
breaks the weirs and falls
breaks the river itself.
[Unsaid. Unheard]

And the dead are piling up in the spaces between the displays – striped sweaters, checked shirts, cashmere scarves, patent leather handbags. Ancient wrinkled deads that sailed here, emptied shtetls, Tipperarys, slave ships. We squeeze past spectres packed like gauzy curtain displays in the Crazy Mare Mall in Patersin, a disused silk mill where bargains are attained. Malignant smell in the mill, in the Passaic River rushing beside. Anne Klein winter jackets, frilly shirts, practical cardigans, ladies' slacks and pleated skirts – racks and racks extending infinitely in the dark brick mill – where New Jersey denizens get their gear at keen prices.

A single-armed, un-alive lady fingers designer fabrics, as she regards the beings that are still living, the energy they put in the buying act. Her missing arm was ripped asunder in a mechanized jacquard-weaving accident back in the day in the Silk when the mills in Patersin were belching steam, belching finished silk textiles, belching immigrants at day's end.

She sidles up with the bargain-hunting, peppy human beings. Their single-minded gazes are fixed in the bins, in the breezy displays and sample piles, the unbelievable bargains. Perry Ellis is available as well. A red running mare is stitched in the labels, blaring in signs and packaging. We are branded with the Red Mare brand in the mill that became the mall.

17

Shag carpet in mustard hues, resembling barf in my place. A rust and reddish bedspread with white curved bands arranged like waves in the sand where currents have made rivulets. Curtains in the same fabric. High library shelves with cabinets at the base, stained dark walnut. Metal grate in the ceiling that emitted freezing air in summer. Birch branches with green in their arms. All that animated green life – packed in the panes. It was like living in a winter tree, clinging in the branches and taking what shelter there was. Remembering the fullness in the leaf years, the changing textures, tints and scent that had garlanded the branches.

Sunlight played in the barf shag carpet where I lay vinyl-listening at eye level with the shag hair dust detritus particles that snagged in the pile. Sunlight caught in the plasticky clear filaments. Unnatural, sickly textile. The nice natural fibre rug in the den had been fitted when she was in her right mind. When she was well and imagining life as an extended thing. The shag was installed after she'd had X-rays because it was easily maintained and in style. Just get it in there and die.

The stale air in the barf-hued chamber enlivened after we visited the mall with Aunt Reet. The Crazy Mare Mall had Perry Ellis, Liz Clayburn and Calvin Klein. Sweaters in fall. New slacks, skirts, new styles. Tweeds. Ah. Make me new make me new the garments said. Buy me and be changed by me. Be changed.

The mills had manufactured silks that haberdashed wealthy NYC families where my granny Jane had been a maid. But after the 1913 silk mill strike, after my badged grandad had cracked strikers' heads with his billy club, the mills had shifted – in a fifty-year span they became airy brick retail spaces selling designer gear made in China that we in the suburbs craved after we'd ditched 'Red City', its tenements, anarchism and shit status. After we jilted the immigrant mantle.

Paper bags stuffed with purchases crunched up the stairs plunked deep in the shag. Crêpe paper perfume and crinkle. Plastic wrappings deflated with vehement exhales as they were punctured and gave their stuff.

I was cheered by new stuff in sexy swells, a slight shift in the way I felt in myself, a freshness in new hues, textures. I liked flannels, tweeds, graph prints, stripes, Shetland sweaters, *matelassé* anything, alpaca, cashmere sweaters, chambray shirts, gaberdine menswear, eyelets, summer ginghams, seersuckers, linens, winter camelhair, jersey in spring, pelisses any time. Maybe they were a key. Maybe they'd make life like the girls in the magazines. They had real lives while mine in the chamber was vague. The purchases might take me away – but it wasn't very far.

Fabrics helped but remained at my edges. Their pleasure quickly fading. The stuff didn't penetrate, didn't shift seed-me layered in there silent, watching. The way they replaced her a little bit. Her feel-smell-presence. Fabrics were her and they were vehicles that might take me away. Fabrics had sex, that ebbed, that didn't bide. The her place and the sex place weren't distant. Nuzzling her was the start and sex later streamed in that same place. Flinging that humid human nestness further afield was sex's passage in future.

The mustard shag chamber had library shelves, a feature she liked, she that didn't study after age sixteen but that built shelves and squeezed in a degree in library science at her life's finish line.

I recall her returning Fridays after a day at the public library, where she was part-time, with titles I'd greedily read. The case in the chamber had maybe six shelves starting high up near the ceiling and ending at hip height where the shelf widened. Beneath were cabinets. The shelves and cabinet were stained a deep dark black walnut. In the walnut-stained cabinet, behind the walnut-stained cabinet sliding panel, with the circular, brass-lined indent in the timber that held an index finger and let the panel slide in a channel, there were albums (Dylan, *Street-Legal*, CSNY, Stevie's *Tunes in the LifeKey*) and, tucked in the back, that thing wrapped up in paper.

The bundled-up thing was bread-sized and light. Unevenly shaped. It had been in the cabinet since 1969. It had heft, but the American central heating desiccated it. Uncle Ant had cut this turf with a slane in Curraghard. With intrigue I had lugged and stuffed it here. In Ireland with him and his daughters we turned the cut turf and it baked in the sun when there was sun. That the dried earth was burned in my relatives' range was fascinating. Elemental earth burned and spread particles creating an acrid-sweet scent in the evening air that, when smelled, always kindles that first trip 'back'.

Uncle Ant must have seen the charm the turf had with me. 'Why, take it, sure,' he suggested, laughing at the idea, which I was pensive with.

I'd never have asked, never knew I even wanted it that bad. The turf was wrapped in the *Ballaghadereen News*, and at the Great Western Inn, I placed it in my blue Pan Am bag, flew Newark-wards with it.

18

In time back when she lived. When she smelled up the car, when her fingers drummed and fingered the fluted-like-pie-crust Buick steering wheel. When she reached her arm instinctively, braced me in the bench seat beside her every time she hit the brakes in rainy streets. Her presence pulsing, fragrancing the space. Breath-warm car, car where we faced the same way: street signs, lights, suburban streets, Jersey sights like malls, highways, bargain basements. Car she'd furtively park at the side, dig up wild tiger lilies in Wayne and replant in her garden beside the azaleas. Tiger-lily thief. Car where, when smaller, I backseat slept, cheek mashed in the leatherette wetted with my deep-sleep spit. Then we ended up in Atlantic City and Aunt Wally. Aunt Wally the funnest, heartfeltest in the family. Instant happiness seeing her smiling at me in her bullet-bra swimsuit, hearing her Philadelphia accent. Sea-swimming with Aunt Wally the everyday swimmer she was. Then the car warm, sandy. Aunt Wally's clam-pie dinners. Uncle Seán grumpy in the recliner, face like meat, whiskey at his side and Winnie clucking, serving, wiping. Uncle Seán with the insurance firm: Burns & Sparks.

The car was an us-place – she and me, else Dad and she and me travelling, visiting relatives less rich than us in Fair Lawn and Midland Park, relatives that were teachers and clerks and insurance agents and candy sellers, still immigrant-tinged and living with recent immigrants. Dad an executive, which barricaded us away in the white places, tenement- and hue-free we were. The car – the vehicle that bridged us and the relatives severed by the cash difference. The car carried us the distance the cash didn't span. We swam in the relatives' inflatable baths, ate their grilled meats, adults drank their martinis and manhattans in their less leafy tracts with less acreage. They never said there was a cash gulf but there was. It was felt. We visited them; they never visited us. Stranded in the affluent suburbs that were indigent-free. Every minimum-single-acre resident in that suburb-present grew up in a crammed-sibling-bed past, knew hunger, knew handball in the streets, were tainted sepia-tinted, grannies and granddads in dirty rags and need, gruelling sea travels that were unspeakable. Laundry hanging between buildings, ladies peeking behind starched lace curtains. Time passed, wars. The 1950s arrived and wham! in came shiny appliances, marble baths, laundry chutes, minibars, multiple car garages, car-key swinging parties that freaked them, in their disremembering track with its single future-based, cash-accumulating, hue-free path.

Severance. Strandedness. It was felt.

I felt it as a chill in my centre, a slashed umbilicus when we left the relatives' parties in the denser areas and headed back up 208 past the trees. Urban Farms was the suburb name. Passed the club and the lake where the suntan cream slicked the surface in summer. It was like being cut but it was said we were lucky, privileged. It was a time-slice in the American myth-dream and it was pervading. It paved life's vagaries, varieties, uncertainties, eschewals with urgency. That life was a bright, flat, white space that lacked penumbral shades and skins. Darkness in its rich varieties and death as a simple fact didn't figure. It was a klieg-light, leisurely life with big cars, fake ski areas and subterranean IBM missile bases where Indian land had been. Sun-drenched and untrue, it was a ruin in the making.

Art class was where the life was. It was her gift. Every birthday. Mine. Late in the day I entered the piney, sharp turpentine tang that tickled the sinuses. Easels and palette tables – the metal tables printed with rural English hunting scenes that adults ate at while watching TV. A sink where I cleaned my hands in dumped turps. Alban Albert, New Jersey artist, was the teacher. He made landscapes, green-and-white-dappled that sat well in heavy frames, graced the bank managers' and lawyers' chambers in New Jersey. Mr Albert was gentle, instructive, discreet. His craft was in charge. I'd find a painting I liked in a magazine and Alban taught the making craft. I did Dürer's hare. Andrew Wyeth's lightning finial. Cassatt's girl in a chair. Edgar Degas's self-likeness. An Edward Curtis black-and-white Native American with a blanket in ricrac patterns I did in grey pastels.

Time was different in Alban Albert's space, a squarish building in a car park near Franklin Avenue. In my father's discarded grey-white shirt, I carried my paints and brushes in and entered the slipstream. A silent speech began rivering in me. Subject – palette – canvas – subject – palette – canvas. Started with a light pencil sketch. Light because heavy graphite blackened the paint applied after. Then the pigment-feel – gritty Raw Umber, Cadmium Red like warm butter, vibrant, blaring. The pigment-feel at the brush tip, the hue at its height.

There was little talking. Mr Albert circulated. Whatever he said was hushed. He mixed a new hue silently, swished pigments with a palette knife, brushed it up there subtly, a new view. We'd stand back, have a think. Try it again. Little by little the painting built up. He brushed brief liquid lines in fluid pigment, weaving the hare's fur a brush-line at a time. Lamp Black, Burnt Umber, Raw Sienna, Zinc White, thatched lines built up, became hare-like.

I had an innate fluency. I'd sense the hue, what pigments amassed in the nameless shades. I'd test a hue mix and usually arrived at it in the first try. I matched hard and blurry edges with the edges in the picture I was imitating, knew that a bunched-up rag was as much a painting implement as fine-haired Russian sable. I'd brush a tint up there, step back, think. It was a space I sank in like a sea. I relished being in that place with painters beside me but I didn't much set my abilities against theirs. I appreciated what they made, but I existed in myself, didn't have much uncertainty that I can recall. After her death this characteristic vanished. I became a vacillating entity.

Raw canvas was like a light table shining beneath pure pigments – hues blazed unabashedly lit. If I put Burnt Sienna after a dried bluish layer, then Burnt Sienna had its legs cut beneath it. Bleakened. The grey spectrum, all the tints and shades were my native habitat. Then there was the entire predicament deciding what is put beside what. Will it have what it takes? Vying with all that is up there? Will it play its part? Is it yelling, is it underbeing? If it's imprecise, scrape it with a pyjama scrap, chuck it in the metal pedal bin. Maybe just let it sit there and see.

Painting was an undivided self-speech. Language flimmering in my veins. It was talking with my hands, wrists, fingers, eyes, gut, even smell. Ink-derived pigments didn't smell as nice. The turp smell, the linseed, the brush-eye-subject-palette-canvas ballet was inbuilt. She didn't give this as she'd given me talk language, but she enabled it in the art-class gift every birthday. She didn't speak it herself but she saw I had that speech. Maybe it was the way I'd lingered in museums the few trips we'd taken. The Met. The Frick. Whatever. Fact is that she saw it. Saw I. Maybe saw her seed-me unplanted. She didn't fear it, she didn't push it away. Rather, she cherished it. This was a gift.

Mike. Tall, silent, cute in a 70s suburban, middle-class, white-guy way. Aquiline face, lips a little pursed. Played basketball. Had a red car. Might have shared a few sentences with him at the bus shelter at Lenni Lenape Ave and Windmill Drive. Tall, skinny, pimpled. Mike, the guy I liked.

Days spent kneeling squeezed between the armchair and the marble plant stand, my right cheek mashed against the glass at an angle. Single sightline in winter between thin beeches, behind the Katchadarians, where Mike Zwick's garage was. Mike's purply red Mustang might appear then disappear deep in the garage. I needed a glimpse.

The time my cheek was pressed against that pane while my father was at the plant. The time my cheek was pressed against that pane while my father was watching TV in the den. The time my cheek was pressed against that pane while my father was depressed, staring at his knees. The time my cheek was pressed against that pane while my father was gambling in Atlantic City. The time my cheek was pressed against that pane while my father was with the Italian Mafia-lite guys at an establishment in NYC. Time time time time with cheek mashed against chilly glass and a slit eye staring.

My chest didn't flutter, my neck didn't flush when I'd first see Mike Zwick. But his flushed cheeks and bleached hair exerted a zing. Let's call it suitability. Wasn't sex in this extended, awkward teenage fad. I hadn't any fantasies with Mike Zwick's skin, enzymes didn't surge when I was within sniffing distance.

I did imagine being in Mike Zwick's arms, being in Mike Zwick's desires, sitting beside Mike Zwick as he cruised Urban Farms in his red car. I wanted Mike Zwick's eye, being a girl a guy like Mike Zwick liked. A demure girl, whatever, but a girl with fewer issues than I. A girl that liked reading less and used make-up frequently. Actually, a girl in far less pain than I was is what I imagined Mike Zwick liked and that is what I wanted. As well.

When I left my self, at what precise time, I can't recall, but by the Mike Zwick time I can say that I was living at the farthest self-margins and remained rather intact. I pressed against the panes with the same zeal as my spirit pressed against my physical edges. Seeking elsewhere.

My Mike Zwick phase was like smut: ritualistic, secret, slippery, shameful – a fantasy that wasn't engaged with real sex much, if at all. It was self-escape via peering and peeping.

Guys became cars. The pursuit then was: seek the right kind. Dependable, well-designed, suitable. What I really wanted was a guy, a car, us driving far.

The suburb started in an ice sheet that was 2500–3000 feet deep, near Mahwah, New Jersey. The ice began melting and the melt filled cavities in the earth that had been caused by the glacier's great weight. These became the lakes. Gradually plants grew, then animals. Then came human beings. The Lenni Lenape, the Delaware, the Munsee. They called the lands they inhabited Scheyechbi. The big lake we swam in every summer starting in mid-June is cited in the annals:

> 'Ye pond called by ye Indians Michanagrape' which here-after is to be called and known at all times by the name of Christian Pool.'[1]

Early Dutch and English migrants arrived. The natives were killed and displaced in skirmishes, battles and wars until the British ultimately claimed the land and distributed it. In 1948 Newark's chief priest purchased the land as the Church's. In 1958 a Patersin man, Pip Prendergast, acquired the lake and adjacent land. The Prendergasts were a big Patersin family, Irish migrants. They'd made it big selling appliances after the war. Prendergast divvied up the land in single-acre sites. The Patersin successes – the white families that made killings in building, in textile industries, in finance in the city – inhabited Urban Farms in their numbers. Built big places facing the lake. Far away (it was just five miles) were the dirty immigrants, the slave-descendants – all the castes we dumped and said we weren't.

They named the place Urban Farms. Urban because they were Patersin street kids and urban was safe, familiar. Farms in the un-distant past had failed. Farms had meant peasants, mud, penury, burden beasts, sepia grannies and granddads in smudged rags, hunched, battered in huts, famine, disease. Farms were unsuccessful. Farms were unclean. Urban Farms was a new clean thing. Urban Farms residents didn't till the land. They plunked residences. Landscaped the landscape. They hired newly arrived Italians and Hispanics as lawn guys. They didn't get their hands in that dirt. What, are u kidding? They had azaleas in it. Nice trees: silver birches, larches, Canadian and Japanese maples, pines. Kids kicked balls and played tag in that landscape. The lake was a nice blue surface in the view. It was a pretty picture. A leisure land.

The streets that meandered Urban Farms were named after the extirpated tribes that lived in the land in preceding millennia: Pawnee Lane, Apache Street, Blackfeet Avenue. The far-flung plains, western and desert tribes were featured: they had cachet, a 'bit different' was the way it was put. Lenni Lenape, Munsee, Delaware – the actual tribes that had lived in what was current New Jersey – I didn't see any streets named after them. That was realer than was wanted. The land had been actually their place and they had descendants still existing nearby in the Mahwah hills. But they were shunned and it was whispered that they were Civil War-era runaway slaves 'mixed' with natives. They were given the slur-name the 'Jacksin Whites'. Better keep things mythic with faraway tribe names as this created the dreamscape that was wanted. Actual living native beings weren't desired. What was desired were extinct names, the idea that there wasn't a native living in the present. The present was Us (white) and Cadillacs, cul-de-sacs, Little League, swim meets, Sunday mass, barbecues, tennis matches, pancake breakfasts, drunk priests, cutting-edge appliances, mean & frustrated nuns, basketball games, seven sacraments, pets, illicit affairs, Hawaiian Punch. We were a Replacement Narrative[2]. The Natives were the past.

Where Apache Street ended there was a dirt track in the trees. It was the edge. Pete Panzer and the druggies might venture in there. We never went that way. We did veer west, where the tarmac ended, went in by the trees and up a steep hill. There was a nice play place just inside the trees where high flint walls made deep fissures and a fresh stream fell: Buttermilk Falls.

We played and dug up triangular, lithic darts by the handful. We knew that the 'Indians' had made them and attached them by winding sinew in figure eights at shaft ends. They whizzed them at animals and their enemies. Hunting and war. We played hunting and war games. We were in this landscape that plainly said it had been inhabited, in a recent past, by humans wearing animal pelts, tracking and hunting deer, birds and bear. Surveys say there were a few ancient paths that merged in that place. Here we were bumming at the beach till dinner time, swimming in the lake while parents played tennis at the Indian Trail Club, which was a cute name. Parents travelled half a mile in big cars hunting dinner in the fancy Acme at Urban Farms Centre. Fathers earned in the industrial estates near Patersin, else travelled by the PATH train, under the river then arriving deep in the city.

We played in the cigar-scented basement lair that held Dad's bar and the taxidermied sailfish with the wall eye he caught in the Caribbean. Lisa with her wavy tresses fastened with a fastener like twin shiny gumballs. We giggled at rhyming ditties, Dr Seuss and stuff we made up. A few lines caused laughter spasms every time we read them, a cause-and-effect experiment that never failed us:

A very fresh green-headed Quilligan Quail
Sneaked up from *in back* and went after my tail![3]

We created sexual escapades with Barbie, Francie and Ken but we called him Big Daddy Williams. His arrival was always heralded by a jingle, sung with a flabby-lipped and puffy-cheeked Bing mimicry. The pitch went up at the last syllable: *It's Big Daddy Will-YUMS!*

When he arrived in Barbie's and her flat-chested friend Francie's space, the dynamics changed and shit hit the fan. Tempers flared and nude plastic slapped in pretend verbal abuse and sexual experiment.

We giggled.

Upstairs, language was being disremembered. Grannies and Granddads might emit strange guttural speech that was crazy and embarrassing. Get them away! Get them in that graveyard quick! We wanted a new speech. A tasteful talk, beige as the carpets in the hallways and the granite kitchen surfaces emerged in Urban Farms. Sentences were clipped. Chats ended quickly as if every remark was a serve the player failed returning; the 'ball' disappeared in an invisible swale. Bland terms – *great, nice, neat* – bleached speech. Ask and get a quick answer. It was helpful, but pretty dismal as well. An emptiness invaded the very thing that linked us. As language disintegrated, we did as well.

Didn't we all miss the sweetness in speech?

CEASE THAT INFERNAL GIGGLING!

Upstairs she yelled at us.

We, giggling in the basement.

21

The writing turns up the
leaf litter.
Trick is: find the lies.

22

It was an ache in my centre right beneath the sternum, a persistent, chilly, pulsing, digging-at-my-centre ache that stayed and stayed. It had begun circa kindergarten and made frequent belly visits in me all the years after. Way after she died, this queer ache persisted until my deep griefs began seismically shifting much, much later in my twenties, thirties. Eventually it faded and became an infrequent guest in my plexus.

She'd had me checked a few times by Dr Declan the paediatrician and he'd given the all-clear each visit. But the ache always came back. Again and again. It might be half a year absent and then it returned and dug in. Stayed. Always a few weeks minimum, it was quartered in my centre, pulsating its icy pain; it never made briefer visits.

The bellyache in child-me caused crankiness, clinginess and unsettlement. Eating didn't affect it. In fact, as time passed it became apparent that the pain didn't reside in my alimentary areas – it wasn't bubbly and gassy, didn't exhibit the burpy, liquid, messier qualities that intestinal tract ailments exhibited. It was meal-indifferent – I had experimented with different breakfasts, lunches and dinners, and my ache was icily disinterested. Baby aspirin, antacids, TUMS, even tempting parent-induced treats didn't take it away.

It was elusive and fickle; many times, after waking up early in the day, it wasn't present. I'd be sanguine, thinking, wishing that perhaps it had passed, but as the day advanced, the pain increased, winding tighter like a timepiece's inner springs until it was a fisty gnarl beneath the sternum and pained me until bedtime.

Being quiet in my chamber inflamed it. Rather *inchilled* it as it was a bleak, glacial pain that had a deserted, existential aspect. At times it induced a barren nausea, an empty, despairing sickness. Perhaps that belly pain was ancient and preceded me. It felt thus. It felt as if I had ingested a deeply blue, unbiased, generalized heartache that had streamed in my famine-struck family line, that likely streamed in that emigrant suburb's family lines and had been generally suppressed in stability- and finance-pursuit, as if the griefs, tears and realnesses that were in the Urban Farms air and buried in its land had been gathered in a mighty clusterfuck that settled in my central viscera and hammered at my insides.

The single sure remedy was distracting myself: watching TV and films, music-listening, playing in the street with friends, talking, laughing, swimming, running – these activities relieved. Whether the actual pain lessened in these times wasn't ever clear. Maybe they simply sidetracked me. We never knew.

The ache was a puzzle.

Eventually I was seen by a clinic and given barium milkshakes. The X-rays might detect what was up with me inside. The barium was such wretched stuff. Chalky, bluish, metallic, it made me feel like puking but I kept it in. The X-rays said nada was up in the medical sense. Adults at least relaxed when that science-clarity came. I didn't.

The plexus pain icily burned inward. Making a baby shape in my bed and hugging a warm thing assuaged it at times; I was usually given a heating pad, a quilted square item filled with warming electric filaments. Eventually the baby shape's efficacy waned and I'd visualize being drawn and quartered like a stretched martyr in the desire that the ache be pulled apart and defeated.

Caresses and warmth did help. I'd gather my five fingers in a tight bunch and push them in deep between my breasts in the space between the last curved rib attachments and the sternum's end, that place where the heart and lungs are tucked beneath the skeletal structure, where my sturdy-ish frame met my hidden vital tissues. By aiming at the pain with my hands, I gained a little relief. It seemed the pain liked being nearly felt and perhaps a bit unsnarled by hands. In later years that pain place was massaged by entreated friends and paid masseuses.

Even if my psyche didn't register heartaches, my physical self did. The ache seemed a tender place in the generally wall-like me, as if, while my mindful places weren't aware, my skeletal, flesh, muscle, nerve, skin and watery elements were awake. I was a receptacle, a carnal receiver, picking up sepia-tinted, Atlantic-traversing energies. My flesh seemed tuned in at huddled-masses frequency, fielding unseen signals.

My central ache became a familiar part. It wasn't really a friend, but an acquaintance – a harbinger that visited with a message that I was astir in that suburb, that all wasn't well even if its affluent surface seemed fine. My ache was like the bubble in a spirit level, pitching as I tried finding balance in a landscape that tilted at weird angles and didn't settle. I flailed and failed then succeeded and failed again at levelling myself with the skewed angles. Maintaining uprightness meant keeping an inner silence, an inner detachment. At my centre there was a felt absence, an emptiness, a damaged and missing thing that hurt.

23

Dad back after a day at the plant, early evening circa five thirty. Hangs up his hat and camel Chesterfield in the hall cabinet with his twenty grey and dun suit jackets, walks in the den, sits in the *Laz-E-Guy* chair and leans, makes a Thinker-statue gesture, his back hunched, bent arms needling his knees. Then he claps his hands rhythmically, glancing left-right, searching, puffing his cheeks, Bing-like. His resigned sigh lingers in the den air. Might it wake everything up – himself, me, his wife that slipped away while he was at the plant?

24

Patersin was where all were spawned, a city five miles away but it might as well have been five hundred. Patersin was the legendary fatherland whence parents and their friends emerged and shared a special link all their lives: Patersin! Silk city filled with bricks, triple-deckers, bars, grime, crime, Micks, Jews, Eyeties, Armenians, Hungarians, Greeks. Blacks were spectral presences and lived in a riverine place called Africa Side. Sure, African Americans, Jamaicans, Nigerians, Haitians, darker-skinned denizens lived in Patersin. They were banned in the mills, the biggest cash-making places. They weren't featured in the Urban Farms plan. We were us. They were them. We were in flight.

When Newark erupted in civil-rights marches in the late 1960s, Urban Farms parents feared the Blacks'd leave Patersin and attack them in their palaces stranded in green-acre lawns. White flight guilt this was. They shaped Blacks as menacing presences. Their clear message was: stay away. Blacks were the substructure that my parents (imagined they) climbed up. Escaped. Passed. Subdued. Succeeded.

Dads had wandered Patersin in street gangs. The Barracks Gang. The Market Street Gang. Nicknames were de rigueur: Clancy, Mugs, Sarge, Nevvy, Fibber. Dads had had a fun past in the Patersin streets; their talk was sentimental. They hadn't cash. They were in gangs. There was street fighting, rampant racism and underage drinking. By all intents, they were kids in a slum but they'd slap me if they heard me say it. Slums? Blacks lived in slums.

Where they lived was similar but different. Different in what way, dads, I might ask. Just different. Then that tight-lippedness that dads were freely permitted, which meant case shut and talk ended.

Dads finished and didn't finish Patersin High. Many dads enlisted and served in WWII. My dad was in a flagman in the US Navy and learned signals. Dads returned and the GI Bill helped them get a leg up. Their race was already a leg up higher than the darker Patersin citizenry. They learned trades and skills, were hired, earned and made their way. The civil-servant and tradesman dads stayed in Patersin else they settled at Patersin's edges, in the tram hamlets that sprang up nearby. The Dads That Made It Big in Finance in the City and the Dads That Became Executives purchased ranches and A-frames in Urban Farms, which seemed in the far-flung sticks even if it was a mere five miles away. Dads in Urban Farms were made men. Cars enabled their living there. This was the Way Things Went.

Patersin girls talked fresh, made wisecracks at the future dads in the gangs. They were sassy girls in A-line dresses, with curled tresses, natty handbags, chunky heels that lengthened their gams. Patersin white girls weren't as free in the streets as the guys. They stayed inside, were sheltered, peeked behind lace curtains at the passing, strutting men. But after a few beers the girls relented, kissed the guys. Maybe fucked in alleyways.

Patersin girls were left behind when their guys enlisted. They minded their ageing parents and kept the hearths warm in their waiting. Many became secretaries, nurses, teachers and when the dads that weren't killed in the war returned, many Patersin girls had babies and left their careers behind. This created issues later in a fair few families.

Emigrant ships had sailed west with grannies and granddads wrapped in rags and guttural speech and dumped them at Ellis

Island. Pity them. They lacked Patersin! We expunged their past as it was deemed irrelevant. We were leaning a single way: future-directed. We were acquiring cash and stuff, making things better. The Passaic River had a riveted-steel train bridge with a sign:

PATERSIN MAKES. THE PLANET TAKES.

Italians had big families in Urban Farms. There was strange linguistic-surname-descendent math happening there as well: the families with many letters in their last names had the biggest families. The Riccis had twins – Danny and Mary – lived in the cleanest place ever, crazy clean: furniture was all wrapped in plastic, the kitchen was like a surgical unit. Mrs Ricci wielded a steam-cleaner frequently while her dentist husband was in the clinic in Mahwah. The Panzavecchias had twelve kids and a very stern dad, a medic. When he answered a call, he'd say, 'Linda isn't available as she and all the children are studying and will be until bedtime,' implying that we were crude lazy jerks – barbarians at his gated driveway. Implying: SCRAM.

Annie Squarcialupi had nine siblings and she was the baby. They lived high up where Pawnee Drive ended abruptly in a messy dead end with felled trees, dirt piles and a rusting JCB, as if the digger guy that had been slaving away in that steep hillside had suddenly expired and was unreplaced. Their sage-green, aluminium-sided place had a steep driveway that I'd never ventured up.

She was a year behind me in Mary Blessed Sacrament (MBS). Annie was small and lanky like a fawn, all gangly, skinny lines. Her MBS white shirt and pleated navy-blue skirt draped like flags in breezeless weather. Annie Squarcialupi's curved parts were her knees, her head and her dark, tender, very liquid and shining eyes. Her eyes seemed always brimming with tears, which, given what happened, meant Annie's fawn eyes were perhaps prescient. She was a nice girl.

An evening a few weeks after the death in my family, Annie's parents, after a night at the theatre in the city, were killed instantly in a terrible car crash near the malls in Paramus. Pity the babysitter that fielded that late-night call, that wakened the nine children with that news.

I never saw her again after the nun explained why Annie Squarcialupi had been absent a week. We didn't attend the funeral; we had a different (Irish) dentist and I guess my parents didn't travel in the same circles as the Squarcialupis. I later heard they split up the kids and placed them with aunts and uncles in distant New Jersey places.

Slipper slip in time. My smallerself, age eight maybe nine. Scamper in Her green place with the green bed and the little green three-drawer chest. Bras in there. Sixties-style padded bras. Fleshen up Her skinniness. Silky, sheeny. Nabbed a few, crept back in my kid lair. Tried them, minced, admired my biggerself idea. Pleasure. Nipples waking up. Wet between my legs. Fingering. Knew I daren't say. Knew this was mine all mine. Mine. Keep it quiet girl. When waves settle run in that green place get that bra back in drawer quick lest they find. Desire in me. Desiring me.

Way Luke Swistak makes me feel in fifth grade. He makes me laugh. I ask myself if he likes me. Bra-pleasure is deep in the dark me deep deep deep. A secret. Luke-pleasure has me seeing me at a distance. My deep secret me was elsewhere. Islanded. Where did my I skedaddle? When Luke mixed up with me, my desire in the deep disappeared. Luke became big and I smalled.

My Fritz Perls-infused relative said I was *field dependent*, needed reflecting, less time spent self-extrinsically.

But I wasn't a self. I was leaky. Leaking.

What is thy desire's nature? asked the shrink in my future.

Desire? My desire?

MY desire?

What shite are ya talking, Shrinky Shrink?

27

Jimmy Eager was the dad and Squeak Eager was the heir apparent and their empire was called Textile Ink. They set up a plant in the East Village in Manhattan and they hired a genius Czech called Max Plank that built their textile-cutting machines. Max was a whizz, and he figgered the way that textiles might be cut, reeled, packaged and trucked.

Textile Ink was making a mint because typewriters were the craze and inked textiles were needed. The entire eastern US was tapping away at typewriters and using typewriter inked fabric by the mile.

My dad was a returned GI needing a break and Squeak was cruising Patersin searching the Irish and Eyetie slums. Textile Ink needed drivers, engineers, machinists, etc., as their business was rapidly expanding. Squeak hired my dad as a general hired hand. Dad started taking the Patersin–NYC train, grabbing a clam sandwich in the Grand Central Clam Bar as he made his way Textile Ink-ward in the Village.

As the typewriter inked-fabric business grew, my dad grew with the business. It seemed he had a talent with hiring and training guys. He climbed the ranks and became vice president. He hired Nigerians, Venezuelans, Haitians, Lebanese, Brazilians, breaking the racist hiring practices in the Silk back in the day. He'd eschew these guys in public, but in their need, with wives and hungry kids in the picture, his segregated heart ruptured a little. His need – present and past, public and private – met their need.

Need was a leveller. He was a racist and he was a helping hand. What a tangled thing.

The fabric was manufactured in textile mills in Alabama. Then it was shipped by train and Vinnie Fuscini and Ricky Baggali picked it up at the trainyard. The yardage was unwrapped and checked. Any flaws were circled and then patched in the next manufacturing phase. Thick paper tubing, a metre in length, held the fabric yardage. The tubes were glued at each end by Caesar, the glue guy. Then they were cut in maybe half-inch widths – whatever was needed by the typewriters in use at the time. The fabric tubes were wrapped and packed in cases in the shipping area and trucked away. The next phase was the inkers but I never heard where the inkers were. And then the typewriter changed.

> Another feature of the IBM 'Selectric II' Typewriter is the IBM Tech III Ribbon. Enclosed in a snap-in/snap-out cartridge, the mylar ribbon needs only to be changed five times yearly as compared to the 64 changes necessary with the previously used carbon ribbon.[4]

Textile Ink changed and became Squeak Plastic Films Inc. Dad and I visited the sleeping Saturday machines at the plastics plant where Max Plank had devised newfangled manufacturing. Tiny plastic pilules filled barrels and smelled faintly burnt. I plunged my arm deep in the beads, my armpit cradled by the barrel edge, put my face near them, sniffed their inflammable fumes and fingered their strange, tingly, particulate thingness. This was the new mylar film's raw material and Squeak Plastic Films Inc. packaged and trucked that inky material planet-wide. Gyred in cartridges that were then snapped inside Selectrics, these clever plastic films repeatedly struck by metal alphabetic keys enabled my dad's Jaguar V6, my university stints, a Jeffrey Banks dress and many veal piccatas in excellent Italian restaurants.

A dad that Made It Big in Urban Farms was a German-American named Frank Fenstermacher. He and his wife became friends with my parents. They'd have drinks in the basement bar and events such as Swingin' Safari-themed parties where the ladies dressed in zebra and tiger prints and there'd be pineapple juice in the beverages, pineapple slices gracing their drinks' glass edges.

Fenstermacher made a mint because he'd invented bubble wrap: plastic sheets trapping air in bubbles that wrapped fragile stuff. He'd retired early, built a massive glass and dark-stained timber multi-level that was furnished futuristically and was plush, e.g., a sauna and jacuzzi in the back yard. When She was getting cancer treatments, I stayed there but wasn't briefed why I was being displaced. I figured She and Dad were having a minibreak by that Pennsylvania lake they liked. There were Germanic rules at the Fenstermachers', and we were always breaking them. Mrs Fenstermacher, in cat's-eye eyewear, yelled frequently at Ted her kid because his rule-adherence was slipping up. There were lists with duties that had checkmarks placed by them, and I did think there was a Stalag feel in the air.

I slept in a skinny guest bed, a thin mattress encased in a zipped Star Trek fabric. The chamber was sparse – a brushed-steel lamp and a Scandinavian desk – it was easily cleaned but induced bad dreams, disturbed sleep. Things weren't right with Her but all in my family circle were shtum. In the clean Scandi cell, my middle ached icily.

Imagine a river jammed with slim burnt timbers after a fire has raged upstream. A charred sapling glade has fallen in the water making baggy black rafts that flex as the river curves and water advances. The burnt sapling surfaces are matte. They repel river water and have a mute shimmer. This is the picture given when peering at charred vine sticks en masse in an artist's drawer.

Squeaky, gently curving sticks in a bag filmy with charred dust sitting in the easel's ledge. Lightweight because they are merely blackened vine ash, barely keeping a shape. They chime when their bag is gently shaken, a delicate tinkle as fired fine white clay fragments will emit when jiggled.

Charred vine is a drawing material usual in life drawing because with the hand's butt it can be erased, the fingers and the entire hand drawing in tandem and blackening. Charred vine lines are easily amended and re-asserted, and a grey mist is general in a paper where charred vine has been used, a mid-grey tint.

There is a give in charred vine. It nearly melts in the paper as fingers press it. It is a perfect medium if what is wanted is a feeling that the fingers are actually making the drawing, are actually meeting the subject themselves. Charred vine fits in that tight space between finger and paper with little intermediary muss. It captures gesture beautifully. Detail is difficult as charred vine speaks in generalities. It creates three, perhaps five, grey tints and it never makes the deepest black, say the kind that black pastel can achieve. It isn't in charred vine's nature as it is in itself dark grey. Dark grey can't make black. If charred vine were layered and layered and rubbed and rubbed it'd achieve a dark dark grey. But black? Never pure black.

Take a charred vine stick and make an attempt at drawing the suburb, its vaguenesses and sadnesses. There is the retail centre, the Italian delicatessen, pharmacy, supermarket, pitiful bank. There is the tarmac, the cul-de-sac. Find the vulgar architectural angles in the pricey real estate where families abide, the laundry chutes and central vacuum systems, massive juicers and ice-makers, but find as well the inwardness in grasses, the hideaways in culverts, in maple glades, fragrant autumn leaf piles, in the tennis club's equipment hut, the shade it casts. Press hard and make the blackest blacks that can be made in the charred vine shade range. Find the grey tints as well, the kindnesses and tendernesses that were there, that want and deserve being drawn, that perhaps haven't been drawn well, hidden as they might be by a spurned resident's bitterness. Use the fleshy thumb base, smear the burnt vine and make middle greys. Make sure the lake's filmy mists are captured, the way they might snag a dad's heart, take him elsewhere than where he is at present, in his Mercedes hurrying up Lakeview Drive, the early Wall Street train his target. A kneaded eraser can lift the grey values lighter if needed, perhaps where the sun hits the man-made beach, where it glints in the lifeguard chair's white-painted timbers, in the sun flecks reflecting in a tennis-playing lady's Ray-Bans.

– O –

I am as close to you as the dead are close but I'm not a dead one, Oona. People like me – no, people isn't quite the right word, spirit, no, entity, no, shadow, no, double, no, guardian angel, no, banshee, no. Jesus, what do I even call myself? Even myself isn't right as I am not wholly a self without you. Tethered to you but I am not in you. For now there is no hospitable place in the body of yours-ours that could house me. I accept this, stay near – as near as your shadow, though I am not your shadow. Outside looking at you, my other. I see you in English class, elbows on the desk, head cradled in your fists as you watch the second hand circle the clock face, Mrs Schloerb droning on about Macbeth and the witches, The Catcher in the Rye, The Outsiders. *Carrying an armful of schoolbooks to your locker, overhearing the jocks talking – great body but face like a dog – their words sear but you hold it in, carried down the hall in the smelly teenage crowd, one little fish in a sweaty salmon migration. Getting caught up in the big and little boy-girl dramas of after-school cheerleading practice, envying the pretty girls on the team. Or at home sitting with your legs in a W shape on the braided rug too close to the television watching* Match Game *'76 – your mother told you not to sit like that and see, you're still not listening – biding time until your dad gets home from the plant at five thirty when he'll hang up his coat in the hall closet, pour a glass of Dewar's on the rocks and join you in the den in front of the TV for the six o'clock news. At which point you go upstairs to your bedroom and put on Bob Dylan's* Street-Legal *or something. When you get hungry enough you head downstairs to find your dad asleep in the Laz-E-Boy, wake him up and say what about dinner and he says how about Burger King tonight and you head down the hill to Oakland in his cigar-scented Cadillac with Jethro Tull's* Aqualung *playing on the 8-track tape player. He likes the flute. Then back home, him to the ten o'clock news on Channel 5 – Do-You-Know-Where-Your-Children-Are? – and you head up to bed. Sleep a dreamless sleep beneath coverlets She sewed from bedsheets, earth colours in a wavy pattern. What's that sound just now? Oh it's 'Build Me up Buttercup' playing on your clock radio to wake you for school. I'm a hair's breadth away in the mornings when you slip into your Huk-A-Poo blouse and your wide-wale corduroys, tie the laces on your desert boots, drag the brush through your pretty chestnut hair though I know you don't think anything about you is pretty. I know you don't feel me. I know you barely feel. I smell the sweet scent of your frozen waffles heating in the toaster, the microwaved maple syrup and butter scent in the kitchen. Watching you day by day, this pane of time-space between us. If it weren't for that barrier we can't break through you'd feel my every breath on you, watching, waiting, worrying, trailing you down the stairs to Frosted Flakes and OJ at the kitchen table with Dad. Goodbye. Pea coat on, walk out to the bus stop sometimes with former best friend Li-across-the-street though lately not so much because she's started fucking college boys and is now an alien entity – sex-distance, dreaminess, confusion in her eyes. Someone else to lose. Same crew on the bus: Italians, Poles, Greeks, all with a lot of vowels lopped from their surnames to fit in, a few Jews who your dad said not to trust. They're just not like us, Oona. With you through the day, in the Spanish class with the teacher whose minimal activities barely count as teaching. The history class with Mr OK whom you love. The guy has a brain and a sense of humour, gets you to love history. I note the little spark in you in OK's class. I note your Not Deadness, however far away it may seem to you right now. You and learning go together. Mr OK makes even boring old William*

Jennings Bryant interesting. There are weirdos in this class, John Jacobus, artist, gay, original. Ari Feldman, editor of The March Hare underground anarchist paper. Marianne Garfagnini, girl with a good brain and not afraid to show it. There's action in this room, and I sense the little bit of self-stirring. It warms me. 'Cause it's generally cold. School. Bus. Home. Waffles or cookies and milk, Lost in Space, The Flintstones, Mr Ed, I Love Lucy, Burger King or Steve's Wortendyke Inn with Dad. More TV, bit of homework. Bed, Sleep. Then it all comes round again. School. Home. Burger King or Steve's Wortendyke Inn. How was school, Oona? OK. How was the office? OK. Nothing much new. Sigh. Stare at the waiters carrying veal piccata or water pitchers. The monotony. This is called limbo. You ride it out for as long as it takes. Go to keg parties because that's what teens do. Hang out at Nancy's and Cathy's and Susan's, talking about boys and who's going out with who, plucking your eyebrows into slivers of moon, curling your hair just so because that's what white girls do in suburban New Jersey, flirting with boys on the football team and not knowing what the hell you'll do once you've landed one. Waiting for Ken to call and he doesn't call. Will Ken call ever? Ken Ken Ken Ken Ken in the diary. Then Ken calls and he feels you up in Penelope Panzer's basement. Then Ken doesn't call. College boy Timmy Kilcullen takes a fancy to you at The Barn and drives you home after many 1970s beers. Parks his parents' big car in your driveway. Through the leaves of the birch tree in front of the den window you spy your dad in the Laz-E-Boy dozing or drunk or both, the TV throwing violent blue flashes on his slumped form. He hasn't heard the car. Timmy pulls you into the back seat for a kiss because you're so pretty, he butters you up, and you have your first actual sex though you don't even know that's what it is. Just a dry, scraping, painful feeling as he pulls down your underpants, thrusts his big sausagey thing into you, shoots off in a second. So that's it? This is what they're all talking about? I'm following you close as you walk up the path to the front door, your underpants heavy and wet. I shed the tears that you aren't able to shed, kick the shit out of the space that surrounds me, strangle invisible necks of the adults around you that I want to do better. Wanting more life to stream through you though I know that it isn't possible. This, too is life, Oona. Life is also being a stone. Nobody prepared you for this — how could they? You think life is only happy and full-throttle joy, life firing on all pistons. Viable life too can be an obdurate state. I want to speak to you, reassure you that this frozen state isn't forever, that I will come back to you when the time is right. But I can't reach you just yet. I see your despair. I try to snatch it when you're not looking. I send people your way that help. Do you feel your load lighten a bit in those moments? I'm not dead; the dead are of a different order. I'm alive and in a place I can't describe as I don't know where I am. All I know is I'm alive and I'm detached from you. For now. For a bit. For as long as it takes.

3

TEETERING IN MUSEUMS

31

Final year in Lenape High I quit the cheerleading team. Had had
it with the squeaky sweaty splits enacted in the gymnasium, thud-
ding pelvises and pussy skid marks slicking the basketball practice
area, the multiple girl pyramids, cheerless drills, the green-and-
white itchy elasticized gear, the pretending I knew basketball rules.
Ari Feldman – anarchist newspaper man, jazz fiend, sex fiend,
Jewish as it happened – was stunned I quit, impressed, asked me if
I'd see *Annie Hall* with him. I did. We did. We ate Bundt cake and
drank peppermint tea and laughed. He infused me with music:
Bird, Miles, Dizzy, Blakey and Silver, Brubeck and Bill Evans and
Trane, Trane, Trane – we Village Vanguarded, met at the Met,
caught a clarinettist at Michael's Pub, singers in the jazz bar in the
Carlisle, played games like Find the Gentile MD in the Upper East
Side. I learned he liked sex, learned I liked sex as well. We did it.
Did it did it in the dark car in the driveway with Dad in the chair
lit in the distance. We'd hightail it, fuck like bunnies in Mulligan's
field under a star-pricked black sky blanket. In kitchen light, first
date night, Dad had warned, 'He's a Jew, they're different. Beware.
Be careful.' He was circumcised, which meant my lips twizzling
his tip making him crazy making him gush in the place where my
speech came where the chastity belt was. He had thick ankles, a
thick prick – the first I cherished. It went hard under my hand,
never failed. We laughed and I learned laughing is a sex act. I
laughed with him inside me in all the places. He had a mind, liked
that I had a mind and my mind liked his mind, twin minds met

and we were happy in pure mental physical release fucking like bunnies in fields cars sheds parking garages, the sheltered and unsheltered places in New Jersey. A gush blew thru the chastity belt, eluded the teeth trained in strangling gurgling keeping me in in in under wraps. Unabashed life bashed in. In bits.

Sex. *Sexus*. SEX. US. Lifegate.

32

Becky and Jim said it might be fun. A Saturday in summer between semesters with zilch happening. Becky's guy 'Buster' Hymen knew Marc the dealer and, shazam! there were the drugs. Suck the little drug-drenched paper scrap and in a little bit start seeing wacky things. We were at my place when Dad was away. It'd be a laugh.

A bit later Becky and Jim disappear traipsing in the trees, seeing faeries maybe, seeing beasts and blue bluebird flight trails; maybe having crazy tree sex. I'm in the kitchen staring at a tiger-patterned fabric, gnarling, twisting in my eyes. Staring staring ensnared in squiggly writhing lines then I quick exit the present and demand WHEN WILL THIS END? Checking my watch. 2:15:00 then 2:15:30 then 2:16 then 2:16:26 I want the end I want the end I want this ended because the fun is finished and the fear is there fear fear sweat sweat breath breath exit inside here is the squishy lawn grass blades ants a fly where the fuck are Becky and Jim and why are they still in the trees? What is the time? What is time? Tar time. Sticky dreck that sits still. Time isn't passing. I'm stuck in the wacky present. I can't leave this. Then.

A black smudge in the right side. If I peer left, the smudge stays small. If I peer left there is the lawn getting dewy, the darkened cul-de-sac, the unlit lights yet lit. Twilight and air and a black smudge teases my eyes at the right.

I dart eyes right and the smudge bleeds like spilled ink until it is all I can see. Blackblackblackblackblack gash in the trimmed lawn. Yawning and lawning. Inside it is a stuffed scream. Inside it the smudge is darkness immeasurably deep and I am falling in tumbling being sucked in the smut black gash. Then a din a reverb a wail a screech. There is speech beneath the scream, an internal stage whisper in my accent. Faint first then clear in my ear. It is my speech and it says I MIGHT KILL MYSELF.

Then me in a lawn-heap sensing every individual grass blade with a new perspective: That I might separate myself put distance between me and my life. The paper-scrap with lysergic acid diethylamide in it illuminated a rip. A gap in me I felt but didn't see. I have newly seen the deep pit under myself. It has never been apparent that my life is in my hands. I am its engine and if I decide, I can end it. I feel death near. There isn't a death wish in me. But the idea that I might kill myself, that this is simply attainable, within my grasp, is frightening. Capability is frightening. Agency. Can I trust that I'm able? What will happen me (Her deathbed refrain)? Her. Death. This grief heap that I and the drug has prised free. Can I chew, digest this? Maybe this will chew, digest me? Will I fall in this pit? Then distant laughter then nearer Becky and Jim tripping traipsing leaving the trees and crushing grass blades seeing heap-me. What will happen me?

Isn't it great? Isn't it the best fun? Such a laugh, say Becky and Jim.

Heap. I'm tired in a me-pile with lawn beneath and in the lawn the pit the pit the pit. Shit. Didn't figure it. Wanted surface skating evading managing life in bits in sips rather than in fucking giant black gashes in lawns sucking me in. Why didn't they say life had pits?

33

With Becky and her friends in NYC at a tiki-whatever-that-is-themed restaurant called Trader Vic's. I am seventeen. We are eating pu pu platters, sipping mai tais – fruity drinks in giant clamshells with pineapple kebabs and five straws plunked in. Rattan wallpapering everywhere and fake tiki-whatever-that-is masks attached. Becky is getting drunk, laughing, Naugahyde bench warm beneath us, suddenly I feel a big rumble like I am a spaceman in a capsule re-entering earth's firmament, everything in me shaking but my friends aren't aware there's a change, that anything is amiss. My ears plug up, my eyes blur, palms sweat. The muscles in my neck stiffen. I imagine my gullet, saliva running in it. I gulp hard, feel an ear blub. Hear the hiss in my ear. See the sight in my eye. Trader Vic's faux handwritten menu typeface getting bigger and smaller like a lens puller is playing in my eyes. Dizzy spinning me yet my butt is Naugahyde-stuck. Stiff still my face is, but inside is tumult, bedlam. Panting, half-breathing, feeling light, feeling like I am mist rather than flesh, a big gaping distance between me and my friends. Miles and miles.

Curly-haired Becky my friend beside me in the Naugahyde bench but I'm far far far. I make speech, and she listens, but the talk isn't my talk. My lips makes the shapes, my larynx vibrates, speech spews in the air. But I am separated and that talk is a din I emit but my I isn't attached. I'm playing at being there.

They can't sense it, they keep talking as if all is fine. I fear I'll faint I fear I'll rant and rave I fear I'll die I fear I'll get put away in an asylum I fear my head might burst I fear my heart might burst. Panic City. I am a panicking speck drifting. Where did I fit? Placeless, panicking, diminished. My heart is thumping and I'm feeling every breath I take in. I feel the air reach my lung depths and I squeeze it, keep it. Then let the breath rush. It feels thin. I imagine my lungs as deflated rubber water sacs inside my chest. Surely it takes will making them inflate every, what is it, five times a minute? I try disremembering breathing, but then it's even harder. I fear I will disremember breathing and die. Can I be sure that breath will just happen *sans* my will? My tiny will? My infinitesimal agency?

We leave Trader Vic's, walk 59th Street and meet all the faces. Here is a lady with a perfectly square face, greasy red skin, spidery capillaries. A man with skin that is nearly blue-black, a face with features unfamiliar. Blue man, that's black man in Irish. What if I screamed that? A white brunette with straight hair and fake tan, a little girl walks beside her. *Pick me up, Mammy. Darling, in these heels?* A hunched man in a business suit with a strange gait that signals he's deranged. Can I tell by the walk? I see a wild searching in his eyes. They fix me in their sights. I feel the breath in my diaphragm. I pull it in. I push it free. Will I remember my breathing? The next face, a lady with ruddy cheeks and white hair. Her face stretches and signals me, the features rubbery. As if I am a bird flying high in the sky, I spy me beneath in the rabble as a very little thing taking up very little space. A thing that resists being weighty, resists having a definite shape. I see my figure expressed as a shaky, chalky line, like the tracing after a murder. I particle-ize and rise, leaving my figure behind. I'm fumes, effluvium wafting in the ethers with the avian creatures. But in reality, my shaky shape keeps walking, struggling in uprightness. Ethereal, I am tethered, barely present, helium-ed.

Skyscrapers rising up dwarfing and dizzying. Street carts and restaurants bursting with eaters and their multiple mandibles demanding sandwiches, salad bars, greasy burgers, fries, steaks. All the human beings in the apartment buildings packed like bees in hives, beings' life energies mixing in the air with the TV waves, subway rumbles, car alarms and taxis beeping creating a massive built and human hum. Step by idle step I walk the pitching sidewalk assaulted by the city's multiplicity, all the races and languages, the dark beings that are different, unfamiliar, scary, the indecipherable languages. Skyscrapers incessantly asserting their scale: fucking massive. They are steel weights in the sky pressing, pressing in, such presences! I can't escape my small flighty state as everything dwarfs me. Extremely vigilant, marking every threat, I scrutinize the man with slit eyes, the raving lady, the kids in a gang I name 'shifty' in my mind, all my awareness has been me-liberated, is thrust past my self-edges and is in the city itself pinging, swirling, eddying, pinballing. This is hardly walking. It's fumbling, teetering, scrabbling, swaying barely managing erectness, as if the sidewalk were ice. I am a deflated thing perambulating, thinking panicking thinking panicking thinking panicking thinking panicking thinking panicking thinking panicking thinking. Walking the city is barely surviving. Each step is an Everest.

The city invaded and there wasn't any relief as if my nerves were wired in with the vast infrastructure, the electrical, water, gas, sewage and service grids, the cars, trucks, buses, subways, planes. My feet sensed subways thrumming beneath sidewalks, the vast human energy, the myriad feelings and ideas and the dead spirits hurtling in the air. The city's hum penetrated and jangled. I hadn't refuge. My eyes blurred. Maybe my brain wasn't able, my small system crashing within the larger machine. I felt infinitesimal, like a speck, that entity I called 'myself' and sensed when I was in familiar places, I felt that myself puddle and flatten in the city's scale. That myself was unfindable.

The skyscrapers, the huge train and bus terminals induced weightlessness. I levitated. Went up. What little heft I managed ascended skyward. I was heavy in my upper area. Stumbling, bracing myself, praying I'd stay upright, intact. Felt as if there was helium in my veins. NYC magnified my diminutive state. I'd never heard the terms *panic attack, anxiety attack*. This was 1979. I called it my 'head thing'. My diaries detail 'head thing' experiences in classes, at parties, mainly in NYC – especially the subway – which were dire, airless, fear-entrapped experiences.

It wasn't the same in all NYC areas. The typical six-level NYC buildings were human-scaled and easier. That architecture nurtured intimacy. If I struck up talk with a waitress, a man at a chess table, a lady waiting in line, it became better. I'd re-enter life and relax, remembering kindness, lives, dear basic human things. My lungs relaxed, weren't getting exhausted pulling air in.

Much later I learned that this was myself breaking back in – a dismantling, falsities beginning their falling away. That panicking was my system being inundated with feeling after numbness had reigned. But at the time that wasn't palpable. The panic wasn't healing-seeming. It seemed bad, it seemed tumult, it seemed crazy. The single apparent feeling was that I was falling apart.

Psych guy at my higher ed place asked, *What is the link between __na and her flesh?*

My flesh? What is that?

34

Insubstantial and bleached are the terms that describe my inner life in these years. An alive being, yes. Yet such a fragile vessel was the frame that held me. I was like a diesel slick in the sea's surface: many-hued, viscid, shape-shifting, easily carried. Pelagic, I was depth-aware yet surface-skimmed, and unfixed.

There was the Ireland urge huge in me still. Ireland was like turpentine – a life-giving, enabling substance that had been planted in my life by Her that had died. Seeds She gave freely, that I nurtured but that pained me. I wretched at the Ireland idea, its fragrance, yet there was a deeper pull, a riptide that drew me back.

I returned as a university student in September 1980. Cigarette-permeated buses belched diesel fumes. Cigarette-permeated pubs belched drunk, leering men. The 32A Dublin bus was my chief vehicle, taking me everywhere, every day in my student life, a safe capsule (cigarette-permeated).

I lived in a semi-d Dublin suburb with a big family, the Kellys. Six children and a mam, dad and a grandad that lived in the granny flat in the back. I and the grandad breakfasted after the kids had been fed and hurried away by their daily family rituals. Grandad and I were given eggs and sausages by the busy mam, shared tea and crusty bread. He read a massive daily newspaper and regaled me with news items that tickled his fancy. I was as interested in sepia past events as he was. We sat and chatted with the tea steaming in mugs while the mam cleaned the kitchen and, at times, chastised her dad's attempts at setting a Yank straight. I recall I was taken aback by his brazen praise that the Nazis had blitzed England – the same place where my father had been a US Naval flagman awaiting D-Day in English bays – the twinkle in Grandad's eye as he watched what inner thinkings he had caused in me.

During the weekdays, I attended classes at an Irish Studies centre that educated mainly Irish-American kids. J.J.'s *Ulysses* with a J.J. expert, Irish language with a Kerry Gaeltacht denizen, literature with living, breathing writers, the Chieftains played music at a Christmas gig. We were being immersed in a culture that had teeth, that ran deep and ran in me. There was a richness that drew me in. It felt like a cure.

After classes, I walked, still a timid, fear-filled thing, in the streets. I was a beautiful girl with cascading auburn hair in waves and a fresh pink freckly face, clear green-blue eyes, which I habitually averted when met with passers-by, didn't chance what might happen if I caught an enquiring gaze. I was vulnerable, anxiety-ridden and hidden within myself. I meandered Eccles Street and Parnell Square, my Penguin *Ulysses* under my arm, its text filigreed with pencil-scrivened minutiae I'd taken in the J.J. expert's finely detailed literature classes, with the A0-sized sheets he'd distributed, Yank disdain in his bleary, gimlet eyes, displaying J.J.'s gridded writing substructures. In Bewley's, I drank brewed java, the single place it wasn't instant and awful. I admired the Tiffany lamps in the Nat'l Library.

After dinner, which they called tea, I'd sit in what I called the den with the kids and the parents. We watched RTÉ news and after it a big BBC music thing that had new bands every Thursday, which excited the kids. Bands like Dexy's Midnight Runners, Adam and the Ants and The Jam had hits. Margaret Thatcher was the prime minister in England. Charles Haughey pulled the strings in Ireland.

Pale, wide-eyed men with Jesus hair and beards, their skeletal frames wrapped in blankets, began appearing in news clips that autumn. They were in an H-shaped jail called the Maze in Belfast, held in cells that they had smeared with their shit. They had begun a hunger strike and had five demands that'd give them status different than the regularly incarcerated criminals. They were fighting British rule and wanted that fact admitted. Maggie Thatcher wasn't relenting. News clips appeared with her fierce face, her hairsprayed hair helmet, eyes squinting in the cameras' glare, jutting teeth bared as she made stern, intransigent statements.

SMASH THE MAZE graffiti appeared spray-painted in many Dublin walls. I asked the Kellys' grandad what it meant and he spluttered anti-Queen epithets under his daughter's stern eye. I read snippets in his big newspaper after he'd finished with it, especially interested in why they smeared faeces, what did that serve?

In my upbringing, Irish 'culture' had been Bing's album depicting shillelaghs and leprechauns, Aran knit sweaters, whiskey (with an 'e'). Irish realities were far far away. We had escaped them and they were hidden and replaced with kitsch. There was a tale that my maternal grandad had sent cash back, aiding the Irish Republican Army Munster branch, but it was just a tale. That term, the IRA, was a distant thing that had zilch meaning in Urban Farms.

At university, I'd begun nurturing an interest in feminism. The ERA (Equal Rights Amendment) was being advanced, and I was excited by it and writings by Adrienne Rich, Mary Daly, etc. I researched where in Dublin I might find feminist meetings. A sign led me up a rickety staircase in central Dublin near the Trinity campus, a chilly, dark chamber that felt like we were engaged in dirty and subversive activities. We all sucked cigarettes and they discussed buying illegal rubbers in Belfast, taking the Irish ferry when a pregnancy needed ending. Rights we Americans had by 1980 were still ages away here, a yawning privilege gulf between us.

I hitch-hiked Galway and Kerry with a girlfriend, drank Smithwick's ale in half-pint measures, dipped my feet in the thrashing, crazed Atlantic. Made a subterranean pact with myself and Ireland that my surface-dwelling self didn't realize I had made.

35

Speech is a planting but not everything thrives.

William Meredith had a cleft in his chin that was a sculptural thing *cast in enduring materials*. It actually resembled a shapely female derrière there beneath his full lips. His entire face was faceted and carved, *extravagantly pretty*. His eyes were large, blue and steady, hawk-like, a bit Ted Hughes-ish. He had fleshy, lengthy ears, like leathery prunes and sparse, well-behaved grey hair.

We pay more attention to the front end, where the face is.

His speech was reedy, Ivy League patrician with a bass line underneath it. He aspirated the h in 'what', had a NYC accent: *dawg, awf,* said the same as 'paws'. His initials, WM, fit his character in their symmetry, reliability and equilibrium, their visual pleasingness, the steady rhythm made by the W and its upended relative. William Meredith was exceedingly articulate in speech during his entire life even after he became expressively aphasiac in 1983; he had a biting wit yet he wasn't mean.

To be of our own nature is what it means to be kind.

He was the first live writer I met. I'd briefly seen him teach an English literature class when I visited the university I eventually attended. It had impressed me. He had impressed me. The semester after the term in Ireland, which was during my third year in university, I became his student. *Between trees and children there is a resemblance.* It was a small seminar in creative writing held up a rickety timber staircase in Windham, the English department building. Meredith's dusty, library-like cubicle was in the same building, and we'd meet there every few weeks and discuss the crinkly papers with the verses I'd typed and placed in a manila file with my name there in pencil written by William, in his careful, upright script, in the manila tab.

My time in Ireland had been my writing subject. The verses surged unthinkingly, unplanned after I returned. They arrived because I needed them. *A great deal isn't right.* Experiences and sensings that had arisen in Ireland were made manifest in verse language exclusively. There wasn't an alternative enlightenment medium. If I hadn't written in verse, my raw experience'd have been *sans* interpretive means. It'd have vanished and been unremarked, unseen by me. I had been rendered insight-less by trauma. The single channel supplying self-fluency was verse, which seemed as if it were written by a creature I hadn't yet met.

> *Poems are hard to read;*
> *Pictures are hard to see;*
> *Music is hard to hear;*
> *People are hard to love.*

Lacking art, I was dumb – dim-witted and self-blind. Because he was gentle and insightful, I felt safe in handing William what I had written. I put the crinkly typewritten pages in the manila file and slid it in Meredith's cubby, at the English department entrance where the secretary puffed unfiltered Camels, her desk strewn with papers.

> *That's what love is like. The whole river is melting. We skim along in great peril.*

There had been Christina, the wife/mam in the Kelly family. She made my breakfast, did my laundry, asked after me at day's end – she had cared. The entire term I lived with her and her chatty family, I hadn't realized it was the first time I'd been in a maternal milieu again. The fact hadn't dawned in me. Wasn't able.

We need the ceremony of one another.

Yet, in verse, Christina and her busy kitchen, her exacting cleaning and her daily appearance – the strange habit she had, appearing day after day and never disappearing – materialized in my writing. The verse was terse yet there were feelings backed up in the sparse language, between the letters. I didn't perceive this, but William Meredith did. *Reticent yet vivid feeling here*, he'd written in pencil underneath the last line. I'd never really weighed up the term, *reticent*.

reserved
withdrawn
inhibited
diffident
shy
unassuming
shrinking
tight-lipped
quiet
taciturn
silent
guarded
secretive
private
mum

A lot is expected of us, ceremony-wise.

It was a term that had earlier seemed negative, a quality that cheerleaders and influential media characters didn't exude. Yet it felt friendly in the way that Meredith had delivered it, in his gentle pencilled remarks. *Reticent* became imbued with undermeanings and subcurrents that attracted me because they were qualities that chimed with my life and my dumb, unrealized language-sense. A text I'd written had divulged things that were true but that I hadn't perceived in myself. Yet the true things had been perceived by William Meredith. He became a gentle reflective surface.

My nature had been affirmed, which isn't a small thing.

Nothing is unseemly that takes its rise in love.

In my little cubby at the campus mail place, I received a letter in William's hand, asking that I be at his cubicle in Windham at a particular time. We met, and he said that he had taken three verses I'd written, titled them and submitted them in a judged thing. They had received first prize. He expressed regret he hadn't asked me if it was alright. Said he hadn't because he was afraid if he had and my verses hadn't been well received, I'd be deflated. Which was true. But they had. And I was heartened by the prize and further still by his kind gesture. He had extended himself. This was a big learning.

I desired being near William and his beneficent ways. It wasn't sexual – he was a gay man anyway, hadn't any interest in me in that way. Neither did I. He asked if I'd be interested in helping him assemble his archive in the summer. Thrilled, I made my plans and turned up at his place in Uncasville an early Saturday in June in 1983. He wasn't there, which surprised me as he was a very dependable character.

I learned that William had had a severe cerebral incident earlier that day, which rendered him speechless – expressive aphasia is the medical term. His teaching career ended then, and he was nursed by his partner until he died nearly twenty-five years later in 2007. I saw him three times again.

Maybe a year after the incident, I attended a dinner at William & his partner's place in Uncasville with William's student friends, as he'd called us. William was hunched at the table, his wheelchair pulled in tight. His chiselled face had been made extremely unsymmetrical by the lateral paralysis. Yet it was clear his mind was still as sharp and perceptive as ever. He listened deeply, his eyes darting between speakers. Frequently, he'd raise a hand and grunt as he drew lines in the air with his index finger and jabbed it, rather rudely – which wasn't like him when he had had speech – at certain guests. The partner'd interpret until we became fluent with this new physical language William was speaking. He was linking what was said by the guests, drawing invisible lines between their ideas, gathering and bridging the guests and their views. It must have exhausted and frustrated him, especially in the early days. Yet he keenly participated. And he listened.

Later, as he rehabilitated himself, he'd write in little spurts. I met him at a launch a few years later in Mystic and he inscribed sincere and kind things in the shakiest handwriting, very beautiful.

Last time I saw him was in summer 2006 in Easkey, in Ireland, at his friend's place. He had a little speech then, languid and careful. He recited a verse and asked that I recite mine as well. We drank a little red wine and snapped a few pictures and then I left, happy that I'd seen him again, fairly certain it'd be the last time, which it was.

Speech is a planting, but not everything thrives.[5]

36

In a museum in Siena, in an arch-shaped painted timber altar-piece, a skyward angel is zapping the shepherds with starry stuff, her fingers spray metallic rays at them. She is in the sky, branch in her hand gesturing at the shepherds in drab capes, a sunny warmth tinting the purple sky she is set in like a jewel. She has an acanthus ring plaited within her pale hair. Her pink wings are attenuated and thin, with studs fastening the feathers and she's trailing cirrus a bit like a firecracker but calmer. Her right hand gestures earthward, where her mind, where all her energy is trained. She may be in the sky, but she is facing earthward gazing at that sheep pen in the painting's centre. Black and white sheep humps penned tightly. Their faces are hidden. The sheep pen resembles an egg basket draped in a quaint black-and-white check quilt tucked in a Sienese hillside beside lacklustre shepherds tending their meagre campfire.

Walking in museums is a bit like being the metal ball in a pinball machine pinging painting after painting. TILT! The parquet seems unflat. TILT! My breaths are half-lungfuls my head is light and filled with unhelpful messages I feel like a speck in a massive time-space museum machine where can I fit in this art culture beauty timeline? Small me tiny me un-matter me untethered me yet I want this art I want that WHA? Sheep pen. It's a sheep pen, my my can I stay upright and draw it quick? Yes I can manage the pencil drawing quick feathery marks in the little pad I carry in my bag capturing shapes never have I seen such a sheep pen it is magnificent flying angel tired shepherds I need a bench catch my breath maybe my equilibrium. Yes a little rest, I feel myself calming, landing. Leave the museum.

Then get dizzy again in the piazza.

Struggling, staying near the piazza edges seat myself at a little café table beside an elderly, black-clad lady. She squints, regards me as the invader I am – the Sienese have endured much marauding in many shapes and in many eras. Then a breadbasket is placed between us and, tearing crusts, we attempt a chat in fragmented Italian and English. Talk bread and weather. She briefly smiles, her eyes crinkling. I sense my breath reaching my lung depths again. Simple interface with a human being – the medicine in it. I recall Zbigniew Herbert's travel diaries in Italy and France:

> ... *the most pleasant item on the schedule: loafing around, wandering aimlessly, a guest of perspective, looking at exotic workshops and stores: the locksmith's, a travel office, the undertaker's, staring, picking up pebbles, and throwing them away, drinking wine in the darkest spots: Chez Jean, Petit Valet, meeting people ... putting your face to walls to catch their smells, asking conventional questions to check the well of human benevolence ...*[6]

The Met is a bitch. Massive art edifice plunked in NYC, my panic Everest – all that cultural energy. I dared it many times. There were failed attempts when I might make it as far as a painting gallery, but then be beset by multiple sensings that swamped me in their simultaneity: zigzag parquet patterns, resplendent, gilt picture frames that held rarefied canvases gracing each wall, high skylit ceilings edged by egg-and-dart plaster details, smartly garbed museum visitants pacing the gallery seemingly unperturbed by the retinal variety, entirely engaged in calm art-viewing. My particular system wasn't able. There was all the visual raw data plus the cultural heft, the sense that the building was filled with ratified, mainly male, artistic achievements and here was I, an unratified female artist speck. I'd freak and retreat, it all being unscalable.

Success at the Met was the day I made it as far as the Sienese gallery, a blue paradise circle sucking me in. Light in my feet always the feeling like I am untethering, a rising-up half-angel, remembering my breath, remembering this feeling is just an *anxiety attack*, a term I learned, which helps me and isn't helpful. The painting that rescued me was G. di P.'s *Adam and Eve Being Paradise-expelled*. The earth a blue dinner plate ringed in astral blues, then greens, then reds with a terrestrial centre. A map with rivers (the Euphrates, the Nile, et al.) skulking snake-like in a vignette. I'd stand in place, sway a bit, but feel my desire rise like sap and partially displace the anxiety. The viewers pass by me as if I am a sapling planted firm in a rushing river. That map shape appeared in many paintings I made later.

In a mendicant's cell in Firenze, a specially made arched wall is placed where a new friar might sit and view Fra A.'s painting all day and night. Fra A. depicts Christ sitting in a fancy chair, wearing a luminescent white tunic with a white fabric wrapping his head and blinding his eyes, while fragmented human gestures are depicted swirling in the air near Christ's masked head. A discarnate head spits in Christ's face. An amputated arm brandishing a club threatens a beating. A levitating hand threatens a slap. I take it these are men-at-arms executing their panjandrum's directives. In his left hand, Christ cradles a crystal sphere. An intact thing.

The painting tells a tale that instructs me, a parable: fragmented isn't a final verdict – fragmented is as pervading as the used-up alleluias drifting in that ancient Firenze air.

Thrall. Being in a larger capability. In museums, thrall is in megawatt magnitudes. I teeter facing vastness: art culture time quantum space. Italian emergency medics, having rescued and ministered many teeterers in the myriad museums, have dubbed the teeter after Stendhal. The French writer in the nineteenth century teetered as well.

37

It was called a Retreat Weekend. This was the 1980s. Gestalt, primal scream therapy, Wilhelm Reich, free sex – stuff like that held sway. There was bad repressed stuff inside us that needed release. It seemed like an idea, and maybe the unrelenting panic I felt might get released here. And cured. I wanted A Cure.

The leader had white crazy hair, a white wizard beard, was a white man, had had a few wives in sequence, fucked frequently, was an ex-Christian minister. There were twenty-five retreaters, all having a turn in the circle centre when the wizard did his thing with an individual while the set watched. We were in NY State – NYC was nearby and many were city dwellers. Seekers. Therapy clients. Life wasn't giving them what they desired. They wanted change, wanted different things than United States, TV, acquisitive, capitalist culture gave them.

Vegetarian fare was served in the break times. Much bulgur. Zucchini many ways. Cheesy veggie lasagne, peanut butter in vats, dried chickpeas in massive glass jars in the kitchen larder. There was tempeh in the industrial freezer. Meals were made by preceding retreaters that needed financial help. I liked that we all wanted deeper whatever. That seemed real. Decided I'd see what was up with this even if I was scared shitless.

We initially gathered Thursday evening. Trust-building was the aim, creating safety. It began with simply gazing in eyes, in pairs, three minutes at a time. Then switch. Then find a new partner and repeat till all twenty-five members had been gazed.

This had already been hard with humans I knew well. With strangers it was stranger and scarier. Yet at times easier. There were quivering, liquid irises, tenderer than I'd imagined. In either sex. Such vulnerability. I inhaled their imperfect breath and they mine. Perceived minuscule chin and nasal hairs, scars. That a human might let his/her mask fall and be seen. It was a risk. I met many that risked/were risk-willing. I felt they wanted it, needed it, this shedding. They breathed as if in relief, as if this intimate space was a desired place. Why? I felt instructed by this braver kind. I was clueless. But attracted.

After gazing we gathered in a circle and in the middle was a big mat. A single mattress type thing, with a carpeted barrel at an end. That was weird. Didn't get what that thing did. Figured I'd learn later. The wizard leader talked and gestured. He said he'd left the Christian ministry because he'd rather be with the sinners than the saints, which I liked. His first wife had died in his arms after a terrible car crash. He'd been dealt a bad hand and he was still quite alive. Had a deep, guffawing laugh.

He said feelings came in pairs, were dark and light. This was new and fascinating:

fear: excitement
sadness: happiness
anger: strength

It made sense in a way; feelings was a very new subject in my inner life. Still, I was shit-scared and tired. It was late. Finally, we all said night night and retired. Big day next day.

It was called A Trip. We all sat in the U-shaped, matted area and in the centre was the mattress and carpeted barrel-type thing, that strange apparatus. The thesis and regimen that ruled this venture went like this: it began with the wizard-leader lying beside the trippee that was wearing a bandana which blinded him/her. The wizard and trippee deep-breathed till they exited their 'head' and went deeper inside screaming, panting, kicking, shaking, freaking. Then stuff came up in the trippee that needed dealing with – fear, anger, shame, sadness – it all gushed and puddled. If the trippee's anger was huge, the wizard gestured at a few muscly retreaters, and they lifted the carpeted barrel thing, which was basically a well-engineered and insulated, kick-receiving beanbag. They braced themselves behind it. The trippee then shimmied near it, still eye-bandana'd, and kicked it like crazy until he/she was physically spent. Characters were released. Wizard man queried the characters as they arrived. The trippee talked like the character and the wizard quizzed them. What did they want? Did they have messages? A drama was enacted, usually with parents, early stuff, traumas. We all played parts, getting lines that incised and made the tripee dive deeper in their stuff. The trip ended with music that fit the scene and dancing. There were twenty-five trips, twenty-five lives in that weekend. Which was fucking exhausting.

It all seemed crazy. Yet it was a relief. I felt crazy and here was crazy in numbers.

The Trip I remember best: she had black hair like a helmet, thin skin, a thin frame. A white lady. The lady's husband had died. Then a few days later she'd given birth. Their daughter arrived and her husband had departed I think cancer killed him and she was in pieces. She was in bits in the centre. We at the rim watched her shatter. She started yelling at G-d, which made the wizard-leader jump up and grab a big pike with a plastic tip, which was in this therapy dress-up chest. He played G-d the Father while she screamed and screamed – a wail I'd never heard. That screech'd strip paint. It didn't cease. I nearly fucking freaked. It cut deep

deep. He held the stick like a javelin and deep-yelled at her: *I'M TAKING THE HUSBAND – TAKE THAT!* And he stabbed the stick at her. He didn't stab hard but aimed it at her side, the tender vulnerable part, St Sebastian-like. *SEE THAT NICE HUBBY WASTE AWAY AND DIE – TAKE THAT!!* He stabbed again. *I'M MAKING THAT BABY FATHERLESS – TAKE THAT!* He stabbed the stick again. She screamed in pain and grief. She writhed and scrunched up like a fetus. She screamed like he was murdering her. She screamed *FUCK U! FUCK U! WHY'D U TAKE MY MAN AWAY? WHY'D U GIVE ME A BABY THREE DAYS AFTER U SWIPED MY MAN? FUCKING G-D. U ARE A BASTARD!! FUCK U I HATE U G-D!! I HATE U! U THINK U ARE GREAT THEN U FUCKING TAKE MY HUSBAND AND MAKE ME HAVE A BABY AND I FUCKING HATE U!!!! AAAAAGHGHGHGHHHHHH!*

Tears waterfalled in her and made the mat wet. Tears waterfalled in us watchers at the rim. We saw G-d stab stab stab her until she was exhausted. She screamed till she was an empty wraith in the mat centre. G-d the Father had a little break, held his javelin at his side, panting and surveying the field, seeing the lady-puddle in the mat that He'd nearly kilt. The deflated puddle barely breathed. In the mat centre she was practically as flat as the mat. Silence rang in my raw eardrums making the quietness palpable after the curdling screams she'd emitted. G-d the Father with the white beard waited-watched as the lady-puddle lay still. He was thinking. He was waiting.

He called her name quietly after a while. I can't remember her name. Maybe Jane. A plain white lady name. Jane, u hear me? stage-whispered G-d the Father. A whimper happened in the lady-puddle, barely detectable. G-d the Father's knees began crumpling. He fell knee-ward, sinking in the mat/mattress beside her. He put his hand in puddle central, which was just a wrinkled, sweaty, tear-stained garment pile that had been an erstwhile lady.

Jane? It's me, G-d here beside u. U feel me?

Uhhhh-huhhh, flattened Jane murmured weakly. All her fight had left her. The wizard man re-emerged then, the G-d the Father mask melting, his human-wizard visage returning. He scanned the circle. He signalled at a large Venus Genetrix-like lady. She left her place in the circle, crawled, then mat-sat near Flat Jane, waiting. Wizard man gesticulated at Venus a bit. Then she talked.

Jane, it's me G-d telling u I've chucked my sharp stick and I'm here beside u.

Uhhhhhhh, Flat Jane blubbed in the mat.

U are pretty flattened there, New G-d said. *Shall I keep stabbing?*

Nuuuuuuhhhhhhh. Nnnuuuuhhh.

I have an idea. Can I suggest we try a little thing I have in my mind, Jane?

Uhhhhhhhhhhh huhhhhhhuhhhh. Jane's assent was a little bit audible.

With a wrapping gesture, the wizard signalled. Venus crawled beside and dug her hands beneath Jane like she was picking up bed laundry that had fallen. She made her legs in an X, gathered the Jane pile in, and held her in her wide lap like the pietà I'd seen in the Vatican with Her that last trip in Italy. Jane cascaded like that dead Jesus did.

This is me as well, Jane, said G-d the Father/wizard stage right. *U can make me a stabber if u want, but I can be a big lap as well if that's what u'd like.*

The Jane-cascade lay still quite a while. It then curled up a little, making a Jane-curve that wrapped itself in the Venus-lap like ivy. Life was in the Jane-curve, the laundry was animating and hugging. It was subtle yet we all felt it and tears waterfalled again tenderly.

While Venus held a gradually puffing-up Jane, Wizard man left the mat area and in the dance area tapped an album sleeve until a ridged vinyl disc emerged. The turntable spun, the needle crackled and Jennifer Warnes sang, in the high-quality hippie speakers, lyrics by a Canadian Jew referencing a blessed lady wearing blue and white that had magically appeared in France, and that a girl called Bernadette had seen and had lived fervently after seeing.

All in the circle crawled in the middle, put their hands beneath the Jane-pile in the Venus-lap and lifted her high. She was extremely light. We walked her like a Greek sacrifice and held her high and swayed while the music played and plinked and Jennifer Warnes sang the Bernadette tune. Then we made a cradle with all the arms at waist height. Jane lay there in the arm-mesh. We swayed her. Her red eyes quivered silver in her tear-shattered face. She gazed up at the wet eyes that gazed back at her unflinchingly. We were practically strangers. We were adrift, searching, white Americans in a nearly ruined/ruined land trying newfangled ways. All the eyes, gazing at Jane, held a limpid, fragile life that felt like a tender thing I might try tasting, might try trusting.

I said inside: *this is crazy*. I said inside: *this is way fucked up*. I said inside: *this feels realer*. I said inside: *I will try finding realer stuff and try living*.

38

Sienese pigments in jars pestled very fine. Sienese pigments in five jars, carried with me all these years since that first Italian trip. Venetian Red, Burnt Umber, Raw Sienna, Yeller Earth and Terre Verte. When rubbed between fingers the hue spreads and sticks in the fingerprint grain making a beautiful pattern. Pigments need fineness. Like talc, like dust, pigments are at the edge between material and air. With a breath-puff they'd be mist. With water they make a paste, which is usual, but pigment mist as an idea is interesting. As well.

Red earth. It hasn't a scent. In fact it subtracts smells. If there were a stench that needed riddance, this is the stuff. It is pestled earth that applies balm in what reeks. There are things in this life that are anti-scent. Draw up what isn't nice. Yet maintain the same mass, are unswelled by what they retain. Venetian Red pigment achieves this miracle.

Venetian Red pigment emits a muffled thrum, palpitates in the jar. When appearing in large passages in painted surfaces it signals a steady, barely perceptible yet persistent heartbeat. Pacemakers' timings can be interfered with by this dyestuff.

When a camera is permitted inside the eye via a chemically widened pupil, the resulting image is an incandescent Venetian Red sphere: a planet Mars traversed by rivers, synapses, acequias, ganglia, nerves, bridleways, fibres, arteries, paths.

Deep deep in the very skull centre the red eye sphere rests and inside it is the retina, the sanctum, the thing that translates all the red-blue-yeller signals. It's a deeper, darker Venetian Red patch within that red planet, quite undefined and sketchy – pure red fluid material like pigment that isn't yet thinned and brushed.

Venetian red ingests all that flies at it in gulps – a trapping pigment.

When Venetian Red is brushed and spread in a painting, passers-by's knees buckle at such passages. The pigment tempts with urges and desires. Viewers want their skin rubbed with it. Paprika, chilli, cayenne – all nice, perfectly nice particles, but alas, all are less distinguished elements. They lack Venetian Red's specific gravity.

Frankly, Venetian Red wants fucking, all the time, every time, with any willing partner. It wants thrumming, expanding, feeling, laughing, sweating. Venetian Red stays up all night, shimmying, falls in fields drunk gazing at the firmament, feels like a meaningless speck puking in the WC and like the largest, brilliantest thing that ever lived when licked. Is the last happy guest at the pigment gathering.

39

Christ brandishing his red-and-white X flag bursts his way in a warm-grey cave.

A devil painted deep Lamp Black has been guarding the entrance. Just the devil's black-clawed paw and his black spiky tail are visible, squished under the flattened plank that Christ has smacked hard with his super strength. Flaxen, glimmering Christ-light streams in the cave where many desperate humans are waiting with big eager eyes. They have been in there quite a while and are getting antsy. The devil is definitely squished. The devil is FINIS. The trapped humans will escape. They have been in abeyance, which is an unfinished state. This painting was maybe five by seven inches in size and was made by a Master Artist in Siena in the fifteenth century. It is in the art museum at Harvard, and it meant much this painting, in my life.

40

It is always in the physical urge, the material feel rather than in an idea. Urges are imperceptible, are uncertain, blind, guessing, testing searching. Urges create lives the way lives run in Graves' stanzas:

> The butterfly, a cabbage-white,
> (His honest idiocy of flight)
> Will never now, it is too late,
> Master the art of flying straight,
> Yet has – who knows so well as I? –
> A just sense of how not to fly:
> He lurches here and here by guess
> And God and hope and hopelessness.
> Even the acrobatic swift
> Has not his flying-crooked gift.[7]

I landed in Maine at a place called Haystack with the Atlantic thrashing the land beneath where I slept, where we all slept, in timber chambers arrayed against a sea-side cliff. I was there with an urge, a textile tactile pull – making, I wanted making, using my fingers. I wanted threads, fibres, hues, being immersed in a material.

At Haystack we were artists and artists-in-the-making. We were learning and eating garden edibles with the sun shining. We slept beneath army blankets near the sea with its swirling and hissing, its spite, its spate and elatedness. There were blacksmiths, glass artists, paper-makers, ceramicists, printers and there was a weaver named Agnieszka. She had lived in Warsaw behind a mythic metal curtain that separated us and them, that had created much fear and had made us, as children, practise diving beneath desks in Russian-related survival drills, had child-me waking up at night thinking the windswept birch branches scraping at the panes were Russian ladders being placed against the wall. But there she was, un-Russian yet still behind that metal curtain, in Maine, teaching weaving, her hair a white helmet, a sturdy-legged, middle-aged, blue-eyed weaver with her niece, Anya – a better English-speaker – as her helper. Anya was my age exactly.

During the war, Agnieszka and her sister had hidden in trees during winters near Lipsk when living with their anti-Nazi/anti-Stalin parents became life-threatening. (Their father was eventually arrested and jailed in Russia. Then he escaped, ran west and died in the Nazi camp at Majdanek.) A few winters Agnieszka and Anna, her sister, lived in tents in the trees, by themselves, and met their parents near a river at pre-arranged times. They survived (in the current map) Belarussian freezes – Decembers, Januaries, Februaries, Marches in the trees, eating what friends left in parcels by the river in mutually agreed places. Agnieszka never said this; I learned it much later after we had been friends many years, but it was there in her blue eyes in Maine that saw far.

I'd been waitressing, renting an apartment in a big city, teaching ESL and learning Spanish with Central American refugees. In between I'd been playing with textiles, with warps and wefts, dyeing and painting silks, weaving. It was this play that drew me here, by the sea in these timber cabins. As well, in the city difficult feelings were being raised inside me. Unbridled rage, endless grief, self-hatred – feelings that had been stuck were erupting. I had a therapist; she was helping. But I kept meeting a fear-despair clusterfuck. I'd feel sad and angry that I'd been left by Her lacking any farewells, then feel afraid that I was feeling sad and angry, then feel afraid that I might kill myself because I was sad and angry – that's why suicides leave the place and I must be suicidal, I surmised. I didn't want leaving. I didn't want death. But I felt afraid that such sad and angry feelings might cause self-death. It seemed rife in writerartist milieus. I never heard a single being say they'd felt similarly until I read *Anna Karenina* and Levin:

> So he lived, not knowing and not seeing any chance of knowing what he was and what he was living for, and harassed at this lack of knowledge to such a point that he was afraid of suicide, and yet firmly laying down his own individual definite path in life.[8]

In my first week at Haystack, I was depressed. Being in classes and meals with artists and art students was challenging. I felt less than: less assured than, less intelligent than, less talented than, less attractive than, less articulate than, less self-aware than, less creative than, less than less than less than less than.

I was tearing myself apart with the less thans. An inner judge and jury castigated me relentlessly. Whereas at age twelve, in my painting classes in Alban Albert's place, I had had an inner strength, a calm place in my making self that stayed interested and remained intact within me even in a class, it had left me, and I'd been wresting it back in fits and starts since. In that Haystack state I was at a self-mercilessness nadir.

Nearing a despair edge, I cried at night in my bunk in my dim timber cabin, with its ruggedly hewn pine lapstraked walls and the sea's turbulence nearby. I'd taken reading material with me, essays which had been written by T.M., a Trappist priest that had died in Thailand years earlier. He'd had an interest in the East and in linking the Western Church's views with Eastern thinkings. I read it hungrily and underlined unflaggingly in pen and green felt-tip marker until the underlined text superseded the un-underlined text. T.M.'s Cistercian mystic ideas appealed; he used phrases like *fully human and fully real*; he was interested in the secluded, peaceful life, which artmaking required. A sentence I still remember that made an impact:

Genuine love is a personal revolution.

I read and underlined in that single pallet, feeling that T.M.'s thinking aligned with mine, yet there was, as well, a distance, a difficulty, an abstractness, a veil between his thinking and my incarnate being. T.M.'s essays as ideas were reassuring, but they scraped at my surfaces. They didn't get inside me and alter things, which I desired. I desired intense rearrangement. Yet T.M. and the flimsy printed pages were all that I had in that cabin.

I feared I'd wake in the night, descend the timber steps and pitch myself in the sea. I didn't want that. It was the same as my fear when in tall buildings. Even with glass between me and the edge, I was afraid I'd be sucked in the abyss because I saw it, because I knew it was real and many had had that fate – Plath, Berryman: artists I admired.

It wasn't easy being an existential mess when classes were taking place. I was ashamed. I didn't want the drama and scrutiny that might emerge if I shared my despair, made it public. Thus, I began undertaking what I had dutifully undertaken thus far and carried me intact: I attended class.

Agnieszka's class was held in a seaside building with glass apertures revealing the wide blue Atlantic in tantalizing slices. She had tacked up her huge tapestries, which depicted wild fields scattered with flying insects and tall grasses, pears, beets, apples, pickles in jars. Her subjects were mundane, but it was the way her hands depicted things with dyed hand-spun yarns that made them strangely beautiful. Dark blue threads twisted and created a tiny fly in the air. Beneath were harebells shifting in a breeze. Her yarn language had multiple registers. Elegant, even passages were interrupted by crazily twisted sisal shapes that were like barbaric yawps in a chapel. Her tapestries held infinite time – all Agnieszka's attentiveness, all her seeing, was heavily draped in them.

Agnieszka's English was simple but precise. Because her speech was halting, her terms held weight and were pithy:

Not everything that pays is worth doing.
Not everything worth doing pays.

I built a crude weaving apparatus with nails and timber and began a tapestry depicting vegetables in the earth. Buried hues. I did what Agnieszka said. I watched her and listened. As I twisted yarns and attempted weaving gnarled parsnip, beet and garlic shapes, I gradually undid my evening despairings. Things were turning a bit.

Anya, Agnieszka's niece, sat beside me in the class. We chatted. Her English was better than Agnieszka's, but Anya's speech was a sibilant whisper. Her manner was gentle and self-effacing. She was an engineer, had just finished her degree, and was interested in prisms, eyeballs, lenses, refractings – the seeing sciences. She lived with her parents – she was Agnieszka's sister's daughter – in a small apartment in Warsaw in what had been the Jewish slum the Nazis had made. She said when she was little and digging in the grassy spaces between apartment buildings, she and her friends turned up many buried items: ceramics, cutlery, much much rubble – ransacked and blitzed relics. I recalled the Indian hunting lithics my friends and I dug up in Urban Farms. Like me, perhaps like us all, Anya grew up with sad, shattered fragments beneath her feet.

There is no hierarchy in suffering.
—Yiyun Li[9]

Anya and I became fast friends, sitting side by side at lunch, in class, at the picnics with students, in the blacksmith's t'ai chi class. The steep timber staircase that linked the class buildings with the cabins became a private amphitheatre. After dinners we'd sit there talking, watching as the pines darkened, the sun fell and the stars began peeping in the sky. The buffeting sea breezes picked up after dark, but wrapped up in the Haystack standard-issue army blankets, we didn't mind.

We talked quietly, watched the crashing waves where the steps entered the water far beneath us. Anya was a living, breathing being – a new friend – with a very different life. She was familiar with scarcity as a daily challenge: bread lines, vegetable lines, meat lines, medicine lines. Apartments in Warsaw in 1984 were small and rare. Cars were a luxury. I listened and imagined that life as best I was able, which wasn't much. I described my suburb, my life thus far, which seemed mild and insular.

I remember in the dining hall watching Anya eat an entire nasturtium in a single bite with her eyes shut as if she were manufacturing an internal, sensual keepsake that she'd take and unpack in her Warsaw apartment. She was preserving things – I saw that.

The remaining summer weeks in Maine passed in a flurry; artist talks, swimming, weaving. My pathetic cabin despairings had been imperceptibly replaced by staircase nights talking and listening with Anya and weaving dark vegetables in Agnieszka's sunlit class.

That's it. We said farewell and left Haystack. I was never quite the same. The genuine had made an appearance. My life began turning.

41

A New England scene: white pickets, blue skies, green lawns, white-painted everything. A humpbacked hill nearby that threw deep shade in the pines and larches, the birches and maples. Williamsburg paints in silver tubes in a timber briefcase that had been a birthday gift. Pig-bristle brushes in bright, flat and filbert shapes and a palette knife – these filled a timber bay beside the pigments. Linseed and turpentine thinner, pyjama rags – all the gear. I had a cheap canvas backed in thick card in a rectangular landscape shape. A paper palette, with parchment sheets and a thumb puncture. There was a small table easel that suited.

Painting was seeping back in me. Just a start. The urge began in tall grasses near a mica-flecked granite step (a step where I'd met a snake warming herself in the evening sun) and a pretty plant with lithe white petals. Buttercup in the lawn with lupins behind. It was a subject. Starting felt like jumping a yawning crevasse. The turpentine made me gag because it recalled Alban Albert's classes and Her but the trick was just get past it. There was a clear-eyed man in my life then, and it made the difference. When I said I'd never make the leap, he replied the span is just the right size. *Just jump*, he urged. Then he went walking in the hills, which was his pleasure.

The familiar fubble the pencil tip made as it traversed the weave in the canvas. The way the pencil vibrated and jazzed my ulna like the vibes. Thin graphite lines emerged marking where the grass met the granite, curly lines where the white petals cascaded, marching lines where the lupin marched and branched in the picture distance. Keep pencil lines light because the graphite mucks up the first hues, I recalled.

Green was an issue. Green had always been an issue. I remembered that Mr Albert mixed special greens in bulk and tubed them himself. The buttery paint had seemed like an edible thing rather than an art material. It made me salivate as I watched him fill the empty tubes with the creamy green stuff then crinkle and seal the metal. He screwed the black caps tight. Then he'd have all the greens he'd need in the landscape, and it saved him. Yes, mixing green was a skill, a subtle art, a very advanced practice.

There was green in the grass, green in the white-petalled plant, green in the lupins, green in the distant trees but it was never the same green. The grass had a flaxen hue in it, thus cadmium pigments; the taller grasses were straw-like and were better bleached with Zinc White and Jaune Brillant; the lupins and trees were bluer-green, wanted Ultramarine mixed with Viridian. The white-petalled plant's leaves were an in-between green and when I sneaked in Terre Verte, it pleased me. I was finding separateness. Making distinct hues. My eyes flicked between the little scene, the palette and the pigments. Little green patches emerged in the canvas. Time passed. I was fixing issues caused by green.

I stepped away and had a bigger view. It was a green mess. There wasn't any pleasing arrangement, it lacked flair and skill. It didn't seem like a painting. I desired a painting whatever that was. I felt a pit in my centre like I had failed. Began cleaning up.

The clear-eyed man returned and when he saw all the greens he said it was a great start. He said all starts are a mess.

42

Payne's Grey, Ultramarine Blue and Lamp Black laid beneath a watery Burnt Sienna layer. The warm and chilly hues vibrate, set the surface abuzz with reticent thrumming, create a grey that sings. I made a Payne's Grey painting while staring at the Atlantic in Massachusetts. Many years I had been teaching ESL full-time and attending every painting and drawing class at the university's art department. Getting back in that turpentine fragrance and surviving it.

I am called a special student in the art classes, which I can take free as university faculty. I am a quiet, timid presence in the classes. The students are in their teens and early twenties. I am in my late twenties – a minimal difference it seems at present, but then it seemed unbridgeable. The teachers are kind. A graduate teaching assistant says, *I see a painter's heart here. Keep painting.* Simple sentences she furnished little thinking their impact. But her sentences were the difference between me packing it all in and me staying, trusting her if I can't trust myself. I stay. Keep painting.

I haunt the MFA, the Isabella Stuart Gardner Museum, a few private Newbury Street galleries, especially Nina Nielsen's.

In the MFA, I study Manet's *V. Meurent* with her deep, rich black necklace tied high at her larynx. Edward H's thinly glazed darks and the built-up paint in the light parts – I inspect their different thicknesses and get yelled at by the guard. Rembrandt in his attic. Big easel, tiny painter. Maybe five by eight inches. Matisse's summer terrace and Matisse's naked girl with the Cadmium Reds in the shade. Gauguin's massive triptych with its insistent queries: where? why? where?

In Isabella Stewart Gardner's Venetian palace, I frequently visit the Titians and Rembrandt's early self-study with his velvet beret and its lavish feather, twisted silk braid that graces his tunic like a draped gilt snake.

A Vermeer depicts a seated girl playing music with a male player beside her plus a girl singer – all in the middle distance. Between us and them, beneath us all, are black and white tiles in a pleasing, rhythmic pattern gathering sunlight. The blacks make Xs where they meet. At the left a heavy table is draped by a Persian carpet, which is gathering sunlight as well. Its intense reds and blues are scattered in the painting – red in the chair back where the man sits playing an unseen musical instrument, blue in the sheer skirt the singer wears.

My Vermeer in the Gardner Museum was swiped by thieves pretending they were the law. They yelled, It's the law, and the security guards let them in. Then the guards were shut up in a small gallery with duct tape keeping them quiet. My Vermeer is still missing. Plus a Rembrandt seascape I didn't much appreciate but still it's sad it has disappeared.

In Nina Nielsen's gallery I study every painting in every new exhibit. These are artists alive in my time, living in the same city as me. Being an artist is a factual capability and Nina Nielsen's exhibits are evidence. Anne Harris, a beneficent painter that teaches me at BU, has exhibits here. They are self-studies, in a limited earth palette, with a fine, unified painting light. She imagines herself as an aged bride, bags under her pinkish eyes beneath a clipped, silver-blue bridal veil. I inspect the paint-handling, marvel at her skill.

I am an apprentice, again.

The clear-eyed man and I travel in Spain, hunting Gaudí and spending days in Park Güell. I snap detailed pictures, capture the shattered, patterned tiles and paint them back in Massachusetts in pigment and gum arabic. Fragmented ceramics with their Venetian Red edges, deep Ultramarine beside Cerulean beside Alizarin Pink. White filling in the tesserae, Payne's Grey in the darker parts. Starting where I am.

43

The Siena museums, public piazzas, parks, churches and refuges – the Uffizi, the Met, the Frick, the Whitney, Isabella Stuart Gardner's little palace, writerartist talks and interviews plus certain films, writings, paintings and verses, the MFA, Nina Nielsen's safe haven gallery, Harvard's art museums, university lending libraries and archives, letters time-stamped in Warsaw and the clear-eyed man helped fill me in in the calm bits amid the Stendhal issues I had.

44

Hiya Ft Lee
did I say my grief
didn't fit even in the sky?
Meanwhile meat
was carried
by rail.

By the way
I am amazed
I am.

45

Terre Verte is Italian green earth and used as an underpainting beneath light-skinned flesh hues. Terre Verte's tinting strength is minimal but it is stable and quite permanent. The fifteenth-century Italian painting teacher C. d'Andrea Cennini and his disciples painted thin pigments in layers, the dried layers beneath building up each by each, making sure every layer's hue integrity was retained. The separate hues were then received as an aggregate in the viewer's retina. Call it 'eye mixing', a thing Seurat played with but which existed much earlier than Seurat's and even Cennini's time. Eva Keuls says that eye mixing as a painting technique was used by the ancient Greeks.[10]

Eye mixing is where hues make retinal magic in the flesh/brain/nerve apparatus. Primary hues: red, blue, yeller, each a tint that can't be reduced any smaller. Red is red is red is red. Blue is blue is blue is blue. Yeller is yeller is yeller is yeller. In the eye, there are receivers that take in these hues. The eye wants entirety. The eye must find the primary trinity. The eye finds the trinity by supplying what is lacking. Thus these essential pairs:

red + green (aka blue + yeller)
blue + tangerine (aka yeller + red)
yeller + purple (aka blue + red)

Each essential pair finishes the primary tri-pattern: red-blue-yeller. The primary trinity is a big thing. If a single hue is stared at a great while, when the eyes are then shut, the missing hues are seen in the mind's eye. Because the retina finishes what isn't seen. It seems the flesh/brain/nerve apparatus wants the three always united. The essential pairs 'incite … maximum vividness when adjacent',[11] writes Itten, a man, like C. d'Andrea Cennini, that studied hue. But Itten did it in the twentieth century.

It makes sense then that subtracting vividness means taking away a pair's partner. Painting a dead man means Terre Verte *sans* Venetian Red/Umber/Sienna/Umber – anything fleshy and sanguine. Here is Cennini's directive:

> We shall next speak about the way to paint a dead man, that is, the face, the breast, and wherever in any part the nude may show. It is the same on panel as on wall: except that on a wall it is not necessary to lay in all over with terre-verte; it is enough if it is laid in the transition between the shadows and the flesh colours. But on a panel lay it in as usual, as you were taught for a coloured or live face; and shade it with the same verdaccio, as usual. And do not apply any pink at all, because a dead person has no colour.[12]

At times green means dead. At times green means new life. As English language learners will say, 'It's depend.'

46

Weeks after my father dies in 1994, I begin gathering the necessary Irish citizenship papers: finding the grandparents' birth, marriage and death certificates. I have a little cash in the bank and I see a chance: I might buy myself time if I play my cards right. I might nab a cheap place and skip paying rent. Increase the time I can spend in art. Lessen the time spent in blindly earning cash. I might find a place in a culture that still values culture. I might matter a bit.

I leave the clear-eyed man behind, Ireland-fated after a sixteen-year hiatus. He is bereft, believes I am having an affair, which isn't true in the usual sense but is true in the unusual sense, which is that I am having an affair with a place.

I am ambivalent re: relatedness and heart matters. Dense, self-blind and self-centred, I am a peril.

He finds he has a grave illness after I tell him I am leaving. I still leave. There is a very hard-hearted thing in me.

4
THE MAW

47

Sky near near, sea-freshness in buffeting gusts, fumbling my way, finally finding Busáras, the bus centre amid dirty streets. I needed the Derry bus but was debussing far in advance. Asked ticket guy if there was a Derry bus but used what I gathered was that city's full name. He nearly bit me. *We say Derry here, miss.*

K! K, just the ticket, alright? Particles in the air. The air feels a substance, hits the skin like a fluid. It is all familiar but it is many years hence. Whiteness in sky, in parched skins, cigarette smells, beer smells, butts, newspapers, chip bags swirling tumbleweeds in the bus centre. Damp smell in the air, the sea, yes, but damp smell in fabrics, in the buses like bad water, like water that's lain and festered and never dried. Musty. Bleary-eyed ticket seller, bleary-eyed bus driver, bleary-eyed passengers, cigarette reek in the WC, sewage back-up in the vicinity, drab jackets, bare legs in summer that isn't summer but girls in sandals anyway, up summer! whatever the fuck blue extremities.

I arrived eventually at the estate that had been creativity-dedicated by the man that had inherited it. He had Irish State-bequeathed it as an artist haven and I and many artists were there making and playing. It was a pile – many-chambered, with a grand staircase, a library, an ancient kitchen. Its facade was multi-fenestrated in wavy glass that had misty lake views, ancient beech and elm views, trimmed lawn and manicured garden. There were cleaners and chefs living nearby that had grannies and grandads that had cleaned and cheffed in that same estate, and they cleaned and made meals that artists ate daily. By the State's purse artists were being fed and given a nice bed.

The rarefied patrician English–Irish air there was unusual and interesting as such places usually are with garden-variety ethnic Americans. But I think it was that place's pervading care rather than its elevated class that penetrated me deeper. Velvet curtains and lace sheers, I learned, calmed the nerves significantly. Sleeping in crisp, bleached, hedge-dried sheets, beneath feather duvets that had been patted and slapped by reddish hands that didn't pull any punches had a salutary effect. As did curved, burnished, bees-waxed furnishings that caught the blurred sky in their surfaces. The daily cleaning and tidying rituals signalled things that had been deprived in my life at multiple levels, care that I missed.

Certainly there was the materfamilias level that was nurtured by the pervasive laundering, dusting, wiping, scrubbing, scalding, bleaching, waxing, baking, frying, washing-up, drying, sweeping, brushing, beating activities that were fervently undertaken in that place. Being immersed in that cleaning hive stirred me, made me miss my female parent that had died, that had been well-versed via her female parent in a particularly Irish cleaning and scrubbing style that was inimitable and was a valuable maid skill.

As well there was a level that I will name the Venus Genetrix level, that is a materfamilias and a creativity level, that by then I was calling back in myself. It was a self-level that, if it wasn't given time and space, might mutiny. Time and space were what the Venus Genetrix was demanding and what the State then was giving artists in that place.

A scruffy salt-and-pepper terrier came with me as I walked the quiet lanes and circumambulated the lake when I wasn't painting. He ran ahead in the alder-sheltered lane then ran back in leaf litter, gave me a quick glance with his liquid black eyes, then ran ahead again. Thus that terrier's distance was twice mine yet he was ever bright and walk-eager every time I came by his place, usually after a late lunch.

A midsummer June night I walked the lawn and viewed the lunar-shining lake. I saw a shining upright thing in the lawn I still can't explain. It seemed like a slightly animate sapling wrapped in white fabric, perhaps being riffled by a lake breeze. But in daylight there wasn't a sapling wrapped in white fabric in that place; in fact, there wasn't any sapling wrapped in white fabric in that entire estate. The tall figure was upright, silent and giving a blurred white light, just there, lawn-standing near me. When I tried walking near it, it disappeared and then there was a massive crashing in the hedge a few feet away. I chased it and guessed it was cattle causing that crash, but there weren't any cattle when I investigated the hedge.

The next day when I said this tale, they said the place was haunted, but I didn't believe in hauntings. I can't explain what I saw but I saw it. I wasn't afraid, but I was perplexed. I wasn't drunk. I guess I'll never understand what I saw that night. Huh.

LIVE HERE. An inside speech yes speech I heard in there. Clear speech. An early sunrise day when I sat by the quiet lake while all were sleeping. Lake mist. Early birds: tits, wrens, a blackbird twirling music in the air. Mist-infused littletalk in me – a speech silent yet accurate as the path a swan carved in the silver lake water. *Live here and die here when my life is finished*, is what it said.

Emigrating in reverse, I faced the headwind that blew the grannies and grandads westward, leaned in, stuck my head in the maw.

48

Leitrim had a nice ring. It had hills, a busy river, the Black Pig's Dyke between here and fabled Up There, the many tales, Them & Us, the Ra, kidnapped nags, Armalites, gelignite, Semtex. It all huddled in the gentle hills and wet, reed-filled fields. I pedalled the hired bike a summer day, left Leitrim village, heading where I hadn't a clue. I was transgressing the map, pushing its limits. The way was quiet, nettled and bramble-fringed. Buildings were sparse. Farmers meandered in distant fields staring vaguely at me as my hired bike ticked by. A few steep hills had me standing, panting and pedalling hard, then I was freewheeling and the village unveiled itself like a quick title sequence as I passed. Sheds with neat turf stacks, wild fields and recently cut fields, silage bales tightly wrapped in black plastic painted with white, chalky, bird-frightening graffiti, laundry lines with pegged underthings and tracksuits, brightly painted walls, electric-wire fences, beech hedges, cypress hedges, habitable dwellings, large and small, scattered here and there. The village was empty at the centre – just a green triangular field in it with cattle whining. The white pebble-dashed church at the field's east end dwarfed everything else, even Murphy's pub and market with Weetabix and End-A-Rat cakes stacked in a farmer-friendly display. I asked inquisitive, massive-headed Jim behind the till if he had ice cream and he sure did: Magnum Classics. I leaned with the bike against the pimply, pebble-dashed church wall, baking in rare, full sunshine, licked up the ice cream, licked the stick and stuck it in the bin.

Passing the bridge, I saw a place with a Farrell's Estate Agents' sign in the garden, sniffed the river air and cycled a few miles up where the main Dublin carriageway intersected. I turned back, re-sniffed the river, passed the Farrell's sign again. Halt, I heard myself say. Halt and think and see. The place faced the river. It was sturdy and single and clean-ish. I rapped the skinny glass pane beside the entry, was admitted by an English man. He had lived there just a few years. Packie McGuigan had built the place in 1948. The inside was bright and airy. Sun streamed in the big west-facing glass. The side garden was belilaced. It had a little Jøtul burner. I'd gather sticks. I'd be warm. It was a beginning place.

49

In the village with the sky and the land. Murphy's field intensely green with cattle whining. The sky grey, white, rarely blue, kissing the green land. And all the gustiness! In gales, the Guinness sign hanging at Rhatigan's pub became a flying beer saucer hanging mid-air. Unreadable disc. The wind crept in all the seams. It blew blew blew blew blew blew even in summer.

That first day in the village I read McGahern's *The Barracks* because the barracks was within spitting distance and all and sundry had said he's an amazing writer. Read him. The family had lived in the barracks with a brutal father and his kindly new wife. She was wasting away with breast cancer. The father was distant. The children, were silently, excruciatingly suffering. This was familiar. The father was a Garda and his new wife was sent away. She was dying in a Dublin clinic and the father was stern, always praying and making them pray, which they hated.

Thou, o Lord, will open my lips.
And my tongue shall announce Thy praise.

The may was ablaze in the hedges, the elder stuck its sexual parts lewdly in lanes and byways that fringed the village. In the distance sheep rhythmically baa-ed and in the garden blackbirds released their intricately tangled music in the river air. Willie wagtails pecked at their black-and-white likenesses in windshields. Cars sped by then braked at the bridge, gaped at the river, then veered left with Carrick in mind.

Inside, I kept reading.

My new dwelling, where I sat reading *The Barracks*, had the penumbral quality I imagine might set up in the retinal chamber when staring, which is strictly ill-advised, at an eclipse. (There was an actual eclipse that first summer. Stunned birds thudded tarmac in weird light.)

McGahern's tale was surely sad. Bleakness and gruelling, empty practices pervaded it. The wife figure emanated meek warmth. She was called a delicate name. There were many finely captured cadences and silences, but I didn't hear them as I read. I skimmed the text, interested in identifying family and place names in my new village. They had said it was a great piece and I must read it. A great Irish writer I wasn't familiar with had written it, and he'd lived right in this village, very nearby.

Such a sad tale, that I knew as a pebble senses its pebbleness. Funny, I travelled all this way, arranged my stuff in different light, in this uncharted village with its chatty mail-carrier, friendly intellectual priest, the badger asleep in his sett in the wild bramble patch beside the bridge, and the empty triangular field in its centre maintaining a green silence. The dark spiky cypresses leaning menacingly near my east wall in the frequent gales. All the rain that plummeted making the side lane impassable. All the breaks in the weather, with that rare sight, the sun. The days the villagers said were fine because they were dry, and I agreed they were fine but initially I saw just grey bleakness. *Thank Christ it's dry* I heard myself eventually repeating.

I dutifully read *The Barracks* in a dual state: partial understanding and primary bewilderment. It didn't yet sink in. My village skills were inexpert, my ear untuned in the particular Irish village unspeakabilities, the embellished speech that misdirects. McGahern's nuances were wasted. The text sluiced by me as river waters gush in the pike's gills and leave the pike in the larger river waters. But I was unnerved and aerated by the text inside. Silent as a pike.

My place was right beside the river. Sunlight blazed in the single glazing. Happiness dwelled in the place. Packie McGuigan had built it, raised girls there, had a teacher as a tenant. They still called it Packie McGuigan's even if Packie and his family had been away twenty years. It smelled like pine, burnt turf, damp, jasmine, river. Under my feet, I scraped away ugly shiny purple deck paint and revealed caramel warm pine planks that captured the sun. Tacked net curtains in the wide glass gashes preventing passers-by seeing in. My place, my light. This landscape was my materfamilias.

A fuzzy red blanket draped the settee back, a deaf white cat curled up in its warmth. It was the highest perch. A tiny Shetland sweater, Stuart Little-sized, dressed the diminutive, headless mannequin that graced the shelf beside the TV where I watched RTÉ and TG4 mystified. Paintings and weavings by friends graced the walls. Things made the place, earthed it. Little altars everywhere. Venetian teacups. Virgin de Guadalupe candles, silver eyes, arms, legs, lungs, hearts – talismans against any vulnerabilities. That little Catalan puzzle depicting Julita, a fifteenth-century martyr with the chartreuse saw cutting her in half, she's grimacing while the saw makes a zig-zag cut in her face. Persian rug Dad snagged during a manic-high minibreak in Turkey – it masked the place the planks didn't meet right. Filigreed Mexican picture frame framing parental picture with Mam jumping, her legs tucked under her A-line dress and Dad gripping her. Legless Mam. That always freaked guests – did Mam have legs, they always asked sheepishly. Mexican water glasses, thick-walled clarities that'd withstand scalding tea and ice water. Matelassé bedspread, ice-blue bengaline curtains muslin-lined, red-and-blue magic carpet in the hall, walls in the entrance painted what I dubbed Fra Angelic Green, a green rarely seen anywhere else.

My village. It will be my village always, even when I'm far away. My village with the river. Yeatsville in the west Kavanaghville in the east what will certainly be Heaneyville in the Up and McGahernville spreading rapidly. The dung-hued finger-shaped signs depicting a quill in an inkwell gauged the high literary qualities in the Irish landscape. I'd watch guests alight their river cruisers, walk expectantly up the path near the bridge, gaze at the blank village triangle. Then, their spines'd slump a little. There wasn't much in the village: a pub, in the distance the big white church, scattered dwellings, the empty centre. It wasn't amenities that made the place, that was certain.

The village's language was backed up in a field. In a field a well was ruined with a dead sheep. An evil being did it with intent. They all knew which he was but weren't saying. Dead sheep in a well will ruin the water perpetually. Glittering shreds fluttered in a tree by the water but didn't greet it. Tied there were keyrings. Were medals with blue ricrac. Were bits well-wishers had in their cars. Plastic Centra bags. Tied there flittering.

The language was in the field; it wasn't in the well. But the well wasn't far. Behind where I lived. I lived near the field. The well was up the lane apiece. All the villagers put the language in the field. In the ruined quarry beside where Lavin gratified his dark need with the children in McGahern's tale. Lavin – they all feared Lavin. They knew what he did but didn't say.

Lavin. The name. And the tale's title. The name is a term. In the term is a field with a quarry. The villagers and the elderly that lived in the lanes dumped all their language in the quarry pit and dumped turf in it. Which is dark but friable and effervescent in its lightness. What grew in that earth was a tuber. The tuber was a term and the term was a name.

What jerk put a dead sheep in a well and ruined the water? The gravedigger said the man that did it was the devil incarnate. We met at the bridgehead, maybe it was New Year's Day when he said it. I said it was blather. Grudges. This side: Fianna Fáil, that side: Fine Gael. He said the man was the devil incarnate and he lived in the village near me.

Yanks knew fridges and appliances. We knew gaits that are big-strided and determined. Yanks didn't meander. We knew children in freshly pressed attire, their gleaming patent leathers like shiny magazine pictures pasted in the grimy newsprint, a summer's day in Leitrim.

They said the villagers were a special breed because their elders had been servants in the Big Place. Being discreet, as they called it, was bred and bet in them. Take all the mum individuals in Ireland – and these were the mummest.

The gauzy mist-rags hang in the dusk, linger well after dawn.
Mizzle that isn't general.
Specific shreds like mist-laundry, hanging.
They stretch a few metres between hill and haw tree.
The rare weather days –
meaning un-rain.
Heaps.
Brush cuttings Francis piles up: thinnings.
Mist-shreds thread near riverbanks
where Hughie hunts mink, the bastards that eat river birds.
It is in these fields I believe the crake was heard.
It was driven away by the tedders.

50

Lined paper scrap lying riffling in the wind. In the little pub car park.

I pick it up; damp as a limp rag and the blue ink bleeds in the printed lines:

Teabags
Butter
Caf nuts

51

A girl's *what* enters the trees first?
Her breath.

52

Myself was water in a glass jar with mud in it that had been martini-shaken and needed settling. Myself had been recently receiving nay had been recently inundated by yes had been recently infused yes had been recently mega-injected with multiple printed pages with language and enthralling images, beeswaxes, ideas, linens, sequences, FLUXUS gurus, sage advice, badger-hair versus squirrel-hair bristles, next new things, 2D & 3D space, false and true premises, techniques, *auteurs*, thinkings, pictures, medium recipes, slide lectures, turpentines and their substitutes, realist gurus, mahl-sticks, garden-variety gurus, verses, falsifiers, art creeps, dreamers, rice paste, pure silver wire, pure silver leaf, patterns, praise, flatness, ancient pigments, HB pencils and kneaded erasers, painty cassette tapes, disdain, minimalists, gum arabic, ancient artists and writers and their lives, NYC gallery- and biennale-grabbing strategies, hues, versifying painters, paintifying versifiers, versifying filmers, filmic versifiers, graphic everythings, Japanese handmade papers, intensities, values, abstract gurus, hard edges, straight edges, blanket dividers, surfaces, geniuses and autistics, metal frames and mats, designs, critiques, saints in caves, saints being beaten by devils, saints in libraries, saints in the sky, saints being visited by angels, saints being burned in piazzas, saints distributing their wealth, saints attending crucifyings, saints being tempted by females (the devil), saints kneeling at infants, saints dreaming, saints attending funerals, saints kneeling by Mary, saints blessing things, saints preaching, saints sharing meals, saints betraying saints, saints gazing up, saints being beheaded, saints being stabbed, saints burning heretics, saints with their spirits being snatched by devils, saints clubbing devils, saints exchanging their hearts with Christ, saints intervening while children are being mauled by animals, saints rescuing the shipwrecked, saints levitating, saints attending a virgin birth, plus shysters, varnishes, drawing pins, Liquin, literatures, space, rancid linseed, rancid rabbit-skin glue, rancid hide glue, stiff brushes, palettes encrusted with dried, caked pigments, painty rags in metal canisters that might ignite.

My edges had remained mainly intact and were retaining the input but there wasn't any sense in it. It was suspended in me, maybe I was suspended in it. I was a brine, a thing being marinated in accumulated paraphernalia but what was the thing being infused with this heady mixture, these artful materials?

At least I was standing up in my kitchen. Filled with swirling particulates. In the village.

Max Beckmann's triptych in the Sackler, its stained-glass hues that pulsated, the greens and pinks, the sharp yellers in the regal headgear, the Egyptian eyes encased in thrashing black marks – I carried them in me, in the mix. Sassetta's sharply shaped water craft, kayak-like, in a malachite lake and lace-fringed, symmetrical trees, perfectly distributed in the Raw Sienna hills in the fifteenth century was as real in me as my electricity bill that was due by Tuesday. As I puttered in my kitchen, demure, mundane still lifes, simple cups and vases lit with shuttered Italian sunlight and painted in Umbers, pale Siennas, creamy whites and lilac blues – these little canvases lingered in the mind while I washed, dried and replaced dishes in presses.

I had painting urges that meant setting up still lifes and seeing stuff and taking my time, marking minute details, splitting shades, hues, greys, intensities. I felt like playing with pigments and mediums, scraping and layering hues and making surfaces that pulsed with light, that were dark as well. I desired scratching painted linen with a single wire and revealing bare linen beneath. I desired cutting things up and pasting them in new arrangements. I desired erasing and repainting. I craved sandpapering painted timber panels and glazing them with runny mixtures. I wanted writing with pencils and charred vine, in the paintings, in pages and printmaking papers, writing alphabets and marks that were language-like. My material-desire was raging.

There were lines in the mishmash as well that swirled in my jar:

We are driving to the interior.[13]

Our woal life is a idear we dint think of nor we dont know what it is.[14]

I must lie down where all the ladders start[15]

her wounds
denying
her wounds came from the same source as her power[16]

I am heavy bored.
Peoples bore me,
literature bores me, especially great literature.[17]

and found only the secular powers of the Atlantic thundering[18]

and these are the forces they had ranged against us,
and these are the forces we had ranged within us,
within us and against us, against us and within us.[19]

Why is Punch crookit? Why wil he all ways kil the babby if he can?[20]

Language images textures making-activities mixed in my waters and I hadn't any discernments except that I rang when seeing/reading/feeling certain things in the mud swirl. I heard/felt the ring, I had a few making/seeing/listening skills that wanted practising. There was a sieve need: I felt like running all these bell-type things that pealed in me in sieving tasks that might let me clarify. Separate things I might use, that might make up an engine that'd get me further. Set aside the things that weren't useful, that didn't vibrate much. Where was I headed? I didn't have a clue. It was my desire and it was a nameless placeless target yet it was real. Elusive yet ringing, calling. An activity that hadn't a definite result, yet felt like life/death if I didn't take it up. It was silent and there was danger. It certainly didn't seem lucrative, this art-related target, yet dividend was its very DNA, in the fluent activity itself. Fluency. I was desiring that. It was safe in that place, that village with the triangular centre and the river near that I might speak.

53

My place beside the river was split-level like the Panzavecchias' ranch-style place where Apache Street and Pawnee Lane met in Urban Farms.

But this was elsewhere, and I was a reverse emigrant, thus my place was reversed as well.

Upstairs was the living eating sleeping level and underneath was the art & writing level.

Upstairs had the glass that was rapped, the electric kettle, the tea bags and bickie jar. Upstairs had the TV, the RTÉ wireless, the Belfast sink rescued in a cattle field in Leitrim, the presses made by the guy in the quizzical van that never called, presses I painted a shade called Gunnysack. Upstairs was wide pine planks and a chimney breast that fit a thin fridge in the kitchen side and a pellet-burner in the sitting side with walls that wept in heavy rain and cried tarry tears that stained the wall sepia. Upstairs had the LED lights strung up by Rudiger after his buying trip with the van in Munich. (He had climbed a chair, severely testing the rush matting's strength under his massive frame.) The lights and their wires grabbed dust and grease year by year, which I wiped with a rag year by year when I felt like deep-cleaning.

Time began changing. I wasn't rushing as much. A day held space, had weight. Time felt ampler. Might the actual actually seep in? I had my senses. There was tea and bread. Burning turf and its ashes. I spent time at the Belfast sink washing dishes and watching cars navigate the tricky bridge. I began identifying cars and their humans. The blue VW was the mailman's. The shiny black Merc was the TD's. The black-and-white bird that attacked my car's sideview glass was a willie wagtail. A thrush smashed a snail shell against the bricks in my garden. I learned that a thrush has a speckled breast, that a wren is a tiny singer with an upward angle in its tail. A blackbird had a yeller eye that pierced whatever it was trained at. Great tits twittered in the birches with high-vis green breasts. Starlings flew in gangs. Nettles stung. Wide-leaved plants in the grass were a nettle rash remedy if crushed and applied in time. In damp places, there were weird grey bugs like little tanks that died and upended themselves. Firelighters, paper and kindling helped light a turf fire. Turf ash was caffè latte-tinted when drenched with rain and wasn't beneficial in gardens. Briquettes were tied with emerald green plastic bands that were burned in grates illegally. Spring began in February. Trees budded in March as did grand stretches in the evenings. A gale was a winter wind. Ice was rare. Washing machines might be kept in unheated sheds. Dryers didn't exist. June days were endless and bright. Electricity was expensive and heated water wasn't instantly available. Kettles were electric. Teabags were large. Dwellings didn't lack fireplaces. Dishpans were used in washing up. Washed dishes were dried and put away immediately after a meal. Time wasn't a usefulness-unit; it was a present we were meant unwrap.

Underneath was Packie McGuigan's carpentry shed. Underneath was like descending in a damp fridge. Underneath is where I did my drawing and painting.

Rives BFK printmaking paper. Nice heft. Takes a beating. Pencil line a river. Rubber stamp eyes in it. Fine line Prussian Blue water-paint dabbed in river. Red squiggle. Nah. Wash white and erase it. Palimpsest it. Finely paint a severed Christ hand Christ leg Christ eyes Christ spit unh unh that's Man-at-Arms spit – the guys giving Christ a hard time in that painting I saw in Firenze that I can't disremember.

Dismember.

Finely draw an eye shape then cut it leaving a space. Take the eye shape and densely write in pen and ink a text in a child's hand then sew the shape back in the drawing with pink silk thread. Sew Japanese rain paper at all the edges. Paint a chartreuse plank with a black devil, his tail and clawed legs squished beneath. Squiggle lines like the Irish rivers mapped by Giraldus Cambrensis then decide they're insipid and whitewash them. Paint a grass patch painstakingly. Take time with each blade, mixing different greens, warm and bluish because time spent like this can be deliberate time and because this grass patch wants a life in this drawing the drawing is saying this the drawing is asking and needs a black black place deep black but diminutive but still determined thwarting all this page-light impeding it because the drawing is seeking balance the drawing wants everything included that is right in the drawing the drawing wants everything excised that is unbefitting this drawing and the way is trying trying things and seeing if they fit and white-washing what's indistinct in the search is precisely the elements this drawing wants in this drawing that is the drawing industry.

It began with a mighty racket in the street in summer: 21st June in fact. I flicked the net and spied three kids pushing a Lidl cart filled with timbers and a kid behind them dragging a shipping pallet green with damp. The big-family Byrne kids, a bit feral and raggle-taggle, started what became a three-day parade. I saw the English weed-dealer's kid dragging a banjaxed Ikea shelf unit with the Garda's grandchildren. The new Nigerian and Latvian kids, attracted by the bedlam, skipped and shrieked and eventually teamed up with Herbert's kids. They all dragged a disused fishing vessel in at least eight parts that Herbert had hacked with a chainsaw. Lapstraked timbers jutted and scraped the street. Rusty nails bared themselves. It was a tetanus nightmare. But the scrappy kids kept hauling and shit that had been discarded in back gardens, sheds and farmyards was unveiled in the infinite midsummer light.

It wasn't just kids that streeled the junk. I saw the pharmacist pass by pulling a water-stained mattress. When they figured what was happening, the Lithuanian car fiends gathered all their deflated, irreparable tyres and wheeled them past, their hands blackening with each metre. Mick Rhatigan's ex-bank manager wife saved renting a skip and sternly directed the kids in dragging away her 1950s kitchen presses plus a dining table and five carvers with ripped leather seats. Travellers' vans, camper vans and builders' vans streaked past and shed stuff. Traffic quadrupled in the village.

In the grassy headland, where the river met the lake, a mighty pile grew. Its base was mainly pallets and the chainsawed fishing vessel. Mattresses skewered by sharp timbers buttressed the pile's sides. Balancing at the pinnacle at least twelve feet up was the battered armchair that had lately been resident at The Crested Grebe's fireside. The pile was artfully assembled, as if by a TV chef assembling a fancy dessert, and the kids lingered at a distance, admiring it. They pestered any passing adult if they had a match. But they were rebuked as it wasn't TIME. Time was 23rd June at sunset. It seemed the kids knew that and were just messing and passing the time till then.

June 23 after tea time, they lit it. A dad had been engaged, and he sprinkled diesel at the base and, standing ten feet away, chucked a lit firelighter and the pile caught fast with flames leaping and licking the mattresses. I watched all this with the net curtain pulled aside. After a few minutes, when the tyres had heated up, melted and began burning, black plumes snaked up and began drifting sideways in the evening breeze. The nearest buildings were the disused Garda barracks and the Bawn. They weren't in burning danger, but they'd be kilt with the black fumes.

Next day, the acrid scent lingered in the village and the embers were still warm beneath the massive ash pile.

56

The place can be described by the unreliable fixer-guy parade that assembled year by year. There was Cian the Barbarian, a plumber. He'd arrive in a van with a 1970 reg, always untaxed. Repaired things as if he were cutting pipes in a cattle shed, trailing muck inside, chucking wrenches and saws every which way. After he left it seemed as if he'd driven in a herd with mucky feet. I cleaned and cleaned after Cian's visits.

Cabinet guy Seán, his address was beside Western Alzheimer's charity in Main Street, Elphin. He'd say he'd be there next week and I'd hear zilch. Weeks and weeks'd pass – silence. Suddenly, he'd be there as if he were expected. At first I tried being direct like a Yank: *where were u Seán? Why didn't u call?* But he was an artful eluder. The lips'd be slack and he'd stare at the ceiling waiting till I melted like an east witch. Anyway, the cabinets were built and installed in time. In Seán's time. I painted them Gunnysack straight away.

The Paddy McCann gutter guys arrived five stuffed in a van like a circus act. They replaced gutters like it was a shell game, the hands quicker than the eye. I was the mark but unwitting. Never knew if they really replaced anything. They slipped away silently and sent a large bill time-stamped in Tubbercurry.

Then Berlin Rainer said he'd never built a staircase but he'd give it a try. Reassured me he'd make it great. The treads were thick and caused trips. The risers were meek. The stairs were a mess. A thick vertical timber beside them fell like a cut tree after he finished.

Nary a screw, a nail attached it. He'd wedged it and prayed it'd stick by magic, atheist that he was. Rainer was a charmer, flirted like fuck, drank tea by the litre, ate bickies by the crate.

57

Maybe the biggest lie we inherited was that sex was an unrent fabric. Sex as this thing that magically fell in a life. Gelled there. Was sacred, came in fully figgered. We'd just feel it, be clued in. Else sex was an animal act learned in sex ed. diagrams. Was technical. There wasn't any learning but diagrams. Sex was deemed perfect. The perfect humans in their perfect marriages with their very first and life partners. It was easy. I get this is a lie at present but back then it was received understanding. The received idea was sex was an entire fabric that we were wrapped up in. We all knew it was there, felt it. We were seamlessly sewn in. The ideal sex acts were gentle flawless lifetime incessant, sustained, sacred.

I wasn't incessant, steady, sustained. I was shifting, fugitive, fleeting, flickering.

Thus I believed I didn't fit in sex. I had much sex that didn't make sense. I believed I was a brazen hussy but I kept at it. Call this learning by living. I felt it as shame. Sex and shame linked in a successful steady sustained perpetual unabating parade. Nevertheless, I persisted mucking in that shame swamp because I needed, wanted.

I began sex as a shapeless bag that was jabbed, licked, kissed, sapped, stuck, struck, held, petted, fingered, flattened, fucked, pinched, sniffed, tied, purred, pinned, pulled this way and that, swivelled, twizzled, thrusted, hugged, lugged. A thing-bag. A thing-bag gradually waking up. Incrementally. Glacially. Harebrainedly.

Clinging, crying, diminishing myself rip rip rip in the fabric. Being small feeling less being abject slavish hammering myself fitting in crevices niches liminal spaces thinnesses less less less. He said I like makeup and tight things, he said pretty up, I like that. I did it and I lessened, my face blurred. He said I like it every day in black lace. I did it when I hated it because he wanted. This guy said I like it when I am underneath and behind. This guy said in the ass and I like it up up there flying and squeeze my nipples hard. These guys all said what they liked again and again what they liked and I was the giver. What they liked was me giving them stuff. That was what I was thinking sex was eternally. Until it changed.

The fabric was all ripped up. I existed in the tears.

Years I battered me. Why was sex hard? Maybe I was ____; fill in the blank. Flawed. Inadequate. Frigid. Hadn't dealt with my shit in therapy. All these nice guys. Me me, the difficulty is me. Years. Meagre sex, meagre desire, them that I didn't desire. Nice guys. Suitable. What is the matter, bitch? Nice hard dicks, wanting pleasing. Veiny. All right in an abstract way. But beauty was lacking. The beautiful were scary, gender didn't matter. Beauty did.

Pleasure islands were markers where real life lay. Actual fun and laughing. Wrestling. Telling him dreams like the esteemed Irish writer, wearing tweed jacket with suede arm patches, and me having sex. Clean sheet perfumes, unguents, being fed peaches by her fingers, Japan tea in a mug. Hair pleasure. Fingering, wrapping, brushing. Way that hair's texture is sexual as paintbrush. A meeting thing. Clean-shaven. Stubble. Tresses. Sex in that. Electric pulses. Eyes meeting beheld. It isn't just thrust but this is what I was taught in the air and the un-talk. Sex was massiver than my mind.

Pelvis shape, her perfect waist, curved clavicle: dun, desert-strewn thing in my bed. Kissing, her skin lava against mine. His sinewy bicep made me shudder. The ice-blue eyes he directed at mine. Way the deep blue iris dark-edges pulsed like a spilled blue-black ink line when he came. Way his eyes quivered. The velvet timbre in her speech gutted me every time I heard her, plucked my sternum, shivered me. When she fingered me, held my gaze, time liquified, became pastpresentfuture. That's where the sex life still hung up. In untime.

Lungs matching the pattern and rhythm breathing deep. My head in her clavicle, lips against her neck, in the warm space behind her ear, tickling in the under curls. The humidity. That tight space and my warm breath makes me snuffle. His skin alert and warm. Eyes flick. He's gazing in mine. Any dreams? Yes, I did, I am a truffle pig kissing his neck, her cheek, her eyes, lips, ear, hair, clavicle, breasts, arm, nipple, snuffling. I wiggle my tail wiggle tail sniffing in the warmth and scent his dark skin. His thumbs at my sacrum, hands winging my waist, pressing pelvic heads, plumbing my depths. Him pacing the bed lifting his paws like a tiger, a-stalk. Unhurriedly, taking my measure with his eyes. With his fingers. After, his lips apart, staring at ceiling, breathing, dumbstruck what-the-fuck-just-happened state.

Squeal and wiggle my curly pig tail, which makes her laugh deep. Snuffling and kissing, I have a very big truffle *SQUEAL SQUEAL* (laugh laugh) wiggle tail wiggle tail, snuffle snuffle, kiss, kiss, I'm digging and eating digging and eating then my hunter finds me and takes it. I'm snuffling, eating all by myself my truffle and I am *SQUEAL SQUEAL* (laugh laugh), pushing aside the earth digging deeper in her truffle skin my desire rises and rises. I snuf-fling the belly, pelvis, thighs, pubes, her delicacy, she squeals, laughs in pleasure and my best terms are a squeal and a kiss and her and I.

The dick I liked, its girth, its sniff, way it waked in my fingers and his tentativeness, he at the end way up there at the bedhead.

Him with the dark eyes with amber street light in the panes. The dick became as rent a thing as the sex fabric I inherited. When I knew he had never let it be held dear. When it wasn't a heat-seeking missile. When it was in bits as well. It became me-giving because it pleased me, this giving. When we felt we were in thrall, in a sex thrall that grew in the ripped depraved places. Because then it was public. I mean it tied me and him in the bigger fabric. We were humbled in its vastness. We weren't particular as much as smitten in a big sex sea tale with a shattered crew. We met in that bed. I felt it might take but it didn't. I splintered and was astray again. This became an entry but it didn't feel like an entry. It felt effluvial. This persisted until it didn't. Then it did again.

58

Regularly I'd peek and see a figure walking the slim path beside my place whatever the weather. Villagers had made it an art: keeping their necks rigid, their wind-grimaced faces facing straight ahead, giving the sense that their scrutinies were singly centred at the landscape ahead. Yet their eyes averted skilfully sideways. Never stares. Never gawks. Just nimble eye-darts that sucked mega-data in an instant. I watched them at this frequently and admired their skill.

The retired army guy was a practised side-gawker. He'd wheel his bicycle by, wearing wet weather gear and an ALDI bike helmet. Facing straight, never turning sideways. Yet when I met him walking near Lavin's, he'd remark that I'd cut back the Leyland cypress hedge under the wall and that he liked the early grape hyacinths that were in the little patch beside the septic tank. *D'ya ever miss America? It's a big change living here.* He grilled me with a subtle, seducing, ex-army intelligence technique. What was his garden-peeping trick? I mused.

The priest's rictus-faced cleaning lady passed by wearing runners and the padded vest liked by many middle-aged ladies – surprisingly warm, matches everything and masks any attractive lady curves. Her gait said, *There is nada interesting either side while I am walking. Everything that is interesting is dead ahead. Such beautiful tarmac! White lines newly painted and very well executed! My white little head rhymes with the white lines. I am walking the street's middle, getting exercise and fresh air, but I amn't seeing a thing, unh-uh*. Yet I'd catch her dark pupils fill the extreme eye edge, her darting glance trawling my place, hauling in as much intel in that instant, details that might be relished later in her private, well-scrubbed priest-helper habitat, might be tittle-tattled a bit.

This made me remember the lace-curtain antics enacted by Mrs Clancy in Patersin that were family tales. She was a meddler, an eagle eye, perched in her triple-decker eyrie. Any hubbub in the street and Mrs Clancy's net curtain whipped back a crack and her beak flattened against the glass. Grimacing, she gleaned what was happening and which bad kids were taking part. Then she'd tell their parents and they all hated her. In Ireland, I learned whence Mrs Clancy inherited her spying genes, but hers were diluted; my villagers were perfected in their secrecy and subtlety, which Mrs Clancy lacked, Yank that she was.

Terence the sheep farmer steered his massively wheeled farm vehicle deftly, unhurriedly, brazenly, head wheeling either side while his starveling farm mutt, hunched and slinking like a hyena, ran behind in jittery figure eights. The height gave Terence views far better than the usual head and car-height views. He was taking it all in indulgently, with pleasure. I wished him well.

59

The Land everywhere: squishing emitting fresh and dirt-like perfumes, being trampled by cattle, sheep, humans, equines, cats, canines, badgers, hedge dwellers, rare red squirrels, pine martens, the hated mink, field mice, little-bird feet, duck and swan webbings, larks' eggs, unharmful bugs and spiders, fleas, ticks, tiny carapace creatures. The Land pierced by hairy nerves, veins, radicles, tubers, tiny pebbles, gigantic pebbles. The Land keeping fed the grasses, trees, hedges – all that plant life sucking water up, feeding synthesizing cells, reaching their plant arms and plant fingers in the sky. The Land gashed by the slane, spade, digger, the pile driver, the JCB, the recently arrived frackers. The green Land, the dung Land, the shining-water Land. Disturbed and piled up higher than the church when estate agents ruled the Land. Diseased Land, plundered Land in the bleak times. Pleated, green, always green, umpteen greens. Ben Bulben a green tea canelé. Sliabh an Iarainn haughty, distant, ever-present flat. A parent kindness in Sliabh an Iarainn. In a Ryanair plane the lakes and rivers were apparent. The Land squeezed in awkward fractals water glinting, skirting. The Land a gem set in silverwater. The Land smelled like water. The living Land ever-shifting. The Land wasn't plunked and static. The Land stirred in itself and stirred us.

Rivers were Land running at high speed; they remembered being as earthed, as sluggardly as Land, but in this life the rivers slinked and raced past the Land like children leaving their aged parents behind. The Sea was-is the future.

We were all in the Land, clutched by it, linked by it. The Land was the thing we shared, smelled, walked, ran. We watched the Sky meet the Land in all the ways it did, in mist and haze in blue sheets that met it in clean breaks, in sunsets and sunrises that existed because the Land met with the Sky. If the Land had been absent the Sky'd just be space and we'd be, well we'd be drifting, wafting, meandering in untethered spaceyness.

The Land had a particular time and a rhythm that was the Land's. I tuned myself and gradually sensed the Land's time, which I didn't ever feel in New Jersey because there the Land just keened and keened. There were recent murders in that Land and the keening was interference in hearing the Land's time, its quiet shifts, the way it settled subtly, dumbly. I guess I didn't find stillness in myself in New Jersey Land.

Land had been Dirt in my suburban child-time. Dirt was digging and making mud pies as if Dirt were put here as material in a play area. We saw nature as we passed it in Cadillacs. Nature wasn't a thing New Jerseyites were well-versed in. Lakewater was a surface watercraft navigated and seemed picturesque in slanted light. Lakewater was a clear substance we practised team-swimming in, winning in. Lakewater held perch and pike that men leisurely fished. In the dense trees beside the cul-de-sac we buried a little timber cigar crate, a time capsule, a future-message. I can't remember what we put in it.

Shallyballybaun was a few miles west where the villagers dug their turf. Summer days I'd lie in the dry-ish heather tufts and nap there. Bears, snakes, wildcats, really creepy crawly things – absent. A few pesky flies, that was it. Being at ease in me. Me and the earth. My weight. Skin drinking in rare sunlight. Breeze, always a little breeze, riffling garments and hair wisps. Breathing *sans* anxiety. Lying unseen, ungazed-at. Lying in that heather sleeping, awake.

Nearby was the freshly cut turf bank. Black black turf. Dark earth, peaty, damp pungent scent. A pit but it didn't scare. A pit I liked. Death might be alright if a pit like this was a grave: springy like a dark bed. I'd crawl right in and stay eternally happily when it was my time.

Fergal McWeeney's turf was stacked, a hundred little campfire shapes drying in the sun. He'd planted spuds, cabbage, parsnips, parsley in the rich turf garden. It made him happy because his da and granda had planted same. It was a FUCK THE EU garden. Fergal's garden staked a claim.

Furze scent, always recalling the Italian girls at the Jersey beaches, suntanning with nut butters. Purple self-heal – *ceannbhán beag* – springing up in the twin-rutted-track-with-the-grassy-middle's edges. Brambles tangling the hedges. Trumpet vine. Fuchsia. Stinging nettles in the ditches. Learning plant names. Medicine itself. Tender and pale birch and alder bark. Scrawled texts there with a sharp utility knife, secret messages I'd revisit every walk. With the years, they'd deepen, blacken. Are still there. I began learning trees: ash, hazel, alder, beech.

Framing. Trussing. Securing. Measuring. Backfilling myself with river gravel.

60

The framing guy made big timber panels that were great painting surfaces. They were nearly square, 48 by 52 inches, because nearly-squares are perfectly imperfect. A timber frame perimetered the reverse side, which braced the structure and made it hangable.

The first thing is rubbing the timber with sandpaper in finer and finer grades until the surface feels silky and is primer-hungry, till the timber gets in a state where it is wanting changed. Then brush the surface with bright Titanium White primer brushing carefully, creating steady, even layers. Then let it dry and sand the channels made by the brush hairs. Then brush again with the primer. Sand again. Brush again. The surface is ready when saliva secretes in the glands in the jaw crux. When a silent *fwump* happens deep in the belly/pelvic area. When the feeling feels like wanting sex when sex feels nice.

The river early in the day in winter is the painting teacher. It says use much turp and start warm, maybe a Raw Umber, Titian-esque wash that will tamp back the Titanium and make the place quiet as the river was when it was early, when Pu'er tea was being drunk. Yes, the surface wants a tea wash first. Then it can think. Then it can tell what it wants next. But it'll take a day drying and in the meantime there is reading and seeing maybe scribbling and music-listening. Making grub. Cleaning. Whatever it is, it is a sinking-in, an inhabiting a place that was lately emptied.

The painting demands a return when it's dry. The first view in the first instant after being away is the treatise the painting has written and is transmitting, which can be received if the tuning is right. It is all in the tuning! And pushing away all the things that are IN THE WAY. This day general uncertainty is the interference. Is this size right? Is paint the medium I want? Will there be cash at week's end? And then the way the uncertainty is handled is the painting's next step. There is a way the uncertainty can translate as a knife that slices the painting's life. Then that is the end. The day is then taken away in distracted stuff and the tea-washed painting hangs there squawking away, but it lacks a listener. The life-quantity spent in averting my ears, in unhearing my paintings, is my biggest sadness. The deluge, the fluent articulacy made by my unattended, just-started paintings! That racket has inundated villages, skies, my basement. It is leaked away life, uncaught.

But then. There it is tea-washed and hanging with little spatters and hue-flecks animating the wall either side, seducing. I sit again, eventually, maybe days, maybe weeks later, bringing myself back in a desire-gesture, with a willingness and a listening. And the painting wants a turpy wash again, but this time in pale blue, which is Ultramarine and Zinc White. I give it a try. Thinly washed and the drying is quickened by Liquin. Bluer here, mixed with Burnt Umber there, shimmering a bit like the river was early when the night had been clear and the land gave up rainwater in a mist. Then wipe it away in places and apply layers, bluish here, umber-ish there. A Raw Sienna passage emerges and sits there, unrubbed away. Asserting itself.

Next day liquid graphite gets a bit nervy. It wants thinned and a big hand-spanned scrub in the left side. It makes a splat, a giant pencil erasure with a lustre. Then a thin emerald line at an edge and the graphite sinks back as if submerged in a river. And days pass in a blur with rubbing and washing, scraping and listening as much as is attainable. These are days when uncertainty is a disremembered blare that has been tamped back – the painting is winning. Happy days when it feels as if a thing is unfastened. The thing likes being freed.

Uncertainty arrives later and asks why and what is the utility? Will this painting when finished just sit in a basement getting damp? Then why make it exist? Then the painting plummets and despairs, asks if it is wasting its time, if it had best vanish and make this a bereft place.

But things change and desire returns. I find myself in thrall again with the painting, asking, being quiet. And picking up a pencil, at an angle at the panel's right side, I scrawl *Write It*. And beside it a sea-green line like an eel shimmying in a river. Because that's what the painting said it wanted.

61

The WC emptied in a cement tank that was slapped up against my dwelling's east wall, by the wildly high Leyland cypresses between me and The Crested Grebe. The septic tank wasn't buried as was usual, as was indeed the law. Instead, it was a little shit shed at the side, pebble-dashed and painted Gunnysack like the rest. The estate agent said that the effluent was pumped in a pipe under the street and emptied in a septic area in the triangular church field. This wasn't natural. Effluent, any engineer will say, likes the descending grades. Any uplifted angle isn't effluent-friendly. But an engineer had inspected it when the sale was made and said it was agreeable. There was a rider affixing the deed as a guarantee. Bit weird but whatever.

The field was a village centre, a picturesque triangle with a church in the apex. The Church Field it was called. A metre-high wall fringed it. The Tidy Village Team had planted beech trees in the paved edges, but the cattle kept munching the sprigs that sprung in spring. Thus there were thin beech stumps in intervals, skinny glum sentinels, guarding the field's perimeter. There were grey patches in the grass where cubist shale sculptures were buried, revealing that there had been a quarry in the field back in the day. A cattle dealer grazed his beasts there. He'd hustle them away in his trailer and they'd end up as steaks and mince after visiting the meat plant in Ballaghadereen. Underneath all this, my sewage gushed and was aerated in buried gravel, aka a septic field. But the field itself wasn't septic until it was.

The shite tank filled up and drained many years and there weren't any issues. Every few years I'd ask the farmer if he'd empty it when he had his slurry tank hitched up during slurry-spreading time. He'd slide the heavy cement cap aside, stick in a big rubber tube and suck the smelly stuff up in the tanker chugging in the driveway. A strange septic arrangement, created by the ancient feud between Packie McGuigan and Mick Rhatigan's father and that was why Mick Rhatigan was the devil incarnate.

Stretching back years, Mick's father had had all the fields within a few miles. A day in 1948 a carpenter called Packie McGuigan asked if Mick's dad minded if he set up a business – just a shed where he'd make turf-cart wheels – near the bridge. It'd be handy. Rhatigan's father gave him a stamp-sized site and Packie built cement-shuttered walls, capped it with undulating tin and that was it. There he had his carpentry shed where he made his cart wheels. He set up a taxi business as well and all was all right.

But what Rhatigan's father didn't expect was that Packie McGuigan was chasing a Keadue girl, meeting her under the dank bridge arches, attending dances in village centres with her and achieving thrills in haystacks. She hugged him at his Yamaha bike's arse end and they were seen everywhere, travelling via Yamaha. Eventually there was an engagement, a wedding and Packie's carpentry shed had increasing spatial needs. He built high cement chimneys, raised shuttered cement walls astride the little walls that had made up his erstwhile shed. Made giant twin glass apertures facing the pub and the church, put a small glass pane at the west side facing the river and the setting sun. It became an actual dwelling, with a shed underneath.

There lived Packie and his wife and eventually their many daughters and the teacher, as well, a renter. This enraged Mick's father. He wasn't expecting an entire Fianna Fáil family plus a teacher in his intimate vicinity when he gave a small land patch away. Mick's father decided making their lives difficult was his life's undertaking. He directed his vengeance in a small strip between Packie's place and the river that was still Rhatigan's (he'd never have given away riverside land). There he let nettles and brambles make a truly impressive, mile-high tangle that impeded Packie's river view. He dumped cement shards, rusted farm equipment, garden and grass clippings, sheep-nut and fertilizer bags, turf-fire ashes – he dumped shit in it. The riverside dump was a perpetual nuisance and agenda item at the Tidy Village Team's meetings. Every 4 weeks a different Team member was given the assignment: Nettle patch – speak with Mick Rhatigan. And every 4 weeks a team member gave the same summary: talk with Rhatigan unsuccessful.

A few years later Packie slapped an unheated cement-stilted shed at his dwelling's backside, the side with the excellent river view. It had a WC, a sink and a bathtub. Then he needed a septic field because shit needs a terminus. Mick Rhatigan's father said The Fuck is Fianna Fáil shite entering my Fine Gael land. Then Packie talked with the Murphys – Fianna Fáilers – and a deal was struck. The shite'd empty in the church field aka the triangular field, under the street.

This is my where-the-shit-went tale. Until the diggers arrived and disrupted it.

62

The villagers knew the current that speech needs. Watching them
talk. In the pub, leaning either side at the bar, their lips met in
the middle and gabbled. In chance meetings in the street. In the
queue in the chapel at the funeral. The deceased's family members
in black in the head pew and all the villagers, their farmer friends,
immediate relatives, teammates, distant relatives in distant places.
Taking the bereaved's hands in their hands and saying that pat
phrase. But never just that. Americans'd have left it at that. But
then there is all the tender talk, sentimental stuff, little tales
featuring the deceased. I remember when she was small and we'd
each carry turf and milk because the master demanded it. And
then the next bereaved, the hand in their hands, the pat phrase:
When I visited him last, he was fit as a fiddle and just after his dinner.
Big breath intake. *He had a bad turn. Awful fast.* Big breath intake.
Squeeze the hands. Shake the head. Then the next bereaved, the
next little kind bit with the gentlest gesture, measured, befitting.

At the bus shelter: *it's very warm isn't it? But there's a sharp
wind isn't there, as well? It's been a fine summer, hasn't it? Last year
was desperate. We're very lucky thus far. Can't whinge, can we? This
bus is a great service, isn't it? I saw Lady Gaga and Queen last year
in the 3Arena. Freddy Mercury was up there in the screen and his
real band were there live. Elvis's actual band with a screen-type Elvis
up there behind them. It was brilliant. And with this bus I was back
in Limerick by midnight. Brilliant.* (She is eighty-ish.) Then an
endless tale: bus mishap, wet sandals and suitcase, cheeky driver,

unhelpful. *We were in Venice if ye can believe it, yes, in June and it'd kill a cat in that heat. And the damp!* Breath intake, quick sideways head shake, eyes raised. *We were glad being back in Ireland. Flying in with Ryanair and the green fields! It's a beautiful place we live in, isn't it? Ah but the rain!* Cluck cluck.

A spit and sawdust butcher's in Carrick smelling with that ageing beef stench. I ask the man with beefy red cheeks and a meat-stained white jacket if he will cut up a chicken. He says he will, walks in the back, returns twice, then three times, dangling chicken parts in my face. The breast split like this, is it? Want the drumstick with the thigh? Isn't a bad day, is it? It is early September and warm, which is typical they say, when the summer ends, the weather picks up, pity the children at their studies. *Yes,* I say, *but my aunt is visiting, and she's freezing.* At that, a larger, even redder-faced man in a white jacket emerges, wringing his meaty hands, chuckling. *The American relative is freezing, is she?* This is making his day. The first butcher demurs, hands me my thin plastic bag with butchered chicken. *Well, there is a nip in that breeze. Can't fault her at that.*

Inbreath, meaning *YES.*

Inbreath meaning *I agree it's bad.*

Inbreath meaning *I'm underlining.*

When a subject wasn't raised, I knew it was really really big. Like when my guy and I split up, they'd give any subject that might bring him in the picture a wide berth, deftly.

What did Neil B. say? Their native language isn't Irish, it's silence.[21]

The mutterings began. I'd meet a villager in the street. First thing pleasantries exchanged. The weather. The news. Then a furtive squint, a whisper. *Isn't it a disgrace what they're planning in that field? Dreadful. It can't be let happen.*

63

Sundays were always the hardest because they were days when it felt as if all Leitrim were at Sunday dinners with their families, gathered at the table and the telly while I was in my place, the Atlantic between me and my relatives, the vestiges. Sundays underlined this self-created exile.

A silent Sunday village. Leitrim were in a big match, and it seemed the entire village had left. I went walking the Cleaheen Rd that hugged the river where it belled and shaped the lake, where sat a single, well-maintained barge that seemed purely pretty. Never saw a human in it. Passed Phyl Walsh's empty place, its carefully planted hedge circles with unruly branches straining against the French symmetry initially intended. Phyl had taught Irish at the academy and was with her granddaughter in the Gaeltacht instilling her with the Irish language. By far the prettiest place in the district, a cherished sense cultivated in it, native slates and timber – PVC was scarce at Phyl's.

The river air felt intensely like air because it was palpable, laden as it was with dampness. That felt air carried the sweet-acrid scent – turf being burned in the vicinity's grates. That scent ever brings back that very first Ireland visit, that initial air awareness. The herby verges, the way the path meandered between the relatives' place and the venerated site where Granny and Aunt Margaret had lived, a hut in a small wet field with a wall dividing it in unequal halves. They'd said beasts lived in the small side and the family in the big side with the fireplace remnants intact.

That first visit we gaped in awe and disbelief at that lithic rectangle, my parents and I making inner arithmetic between the suburb we lived in and this granny-related ruin. It was an advanced calculus that warped us.

My father made a picture with his fancy camera that same day. I'm sitting between relatives in a big raspberry armchair with raspberry wallpapered walls behind us and a glass case with fine china, crystal glasses and Beleek figurines that caused hushes in the girls when they were let peer in at them. The eldest girl and next-eldest girl with their sunburned faces gaze up at my father and in his camera's lens. My eyes are fixed away, at the rug, my buck teeth biting my lip, keeping in my secret pleasures.

I was between new relatives in a strange armchair. They chatted away, asked me things, laughed at my accent and shushed the screeches made by the little girls, their cheeks flushed easily in anger and embarrassment. That we were related, that this else-where was (partially) mine was a relief, but a silent relief that wasn't self-articulable. That I'd carried any burden that needed relieving in the first place wasn't in my awareness then. But there was a happiness in finding a familiar-yet-strange place that wasn't anything like the suburbs, which were all I knew then. My sweet little awkward face, aged eight, is bewildered and arrived. If I didn't yet raise my small face at the camera with my relatives' casual ease, at least I smiled within myself. If I didn't yet participate in all the fun, at least I was seated near, in their midst.

Re-entering the village that Sunday after the Cleaheen Rd was as if I were descending a watery ash-and-elder heaven and entering an architecture-trading-and-begrudgery village: the church, pubs, a few scattered dwellings and Murphy's triangular field in the centre. I neared my place, walking between Mick Rhatigan's ancient pub, The Crested Grebe, and the flashy twenty-first-century-aiming minimart at the right. Running the gauntlet. Passed a red-haired man with a pick and a gravelly tarmacadam pile. He ceased tapping his pick and saluted and I saluted back. I walked up my steps and went in. The clanging pickaxe resumed.

Next day and I'm getting my milk in Mary's Centra. Mary is abubble with excitement. *Did u see that fella with the pickaxe in the street yesterday? Well, I did in fact. U DID? Michael, she saw that fella in the street!*

Her husband, steaming tea cup in hand, walks in the minimart, leaving the adjacent kitchen. Blurt the tale: red-haired man, quiet village, pickaxe, clanging. Mary is bursting with excitement. Michael, hear this? She saw it, she says she saw it. We'll call the TD with this. She tells me that Mick Rhatigan has redirected the rainwater by hiring a red-haired man and building an illegal ramp in the street – they did it Sunday, when the village is empty, away at the match final. We spy the illegal ramp, a big tarry black pimple in the street.

Mary's ecstasy at my blurt was remarkable. I'd given brazen evidence that hampered a shady trick Rhatigan had nearly success-fully executed. She'd call the TD and tell him she had evidence. She'd nab the culprit. This gave her much glee. Next week the red-haired man was back scraping away the ramp, a sheepish aspect in his gestures. Mick Rhatigan was glaringly absent all week.

The unsaid but highly present speech and silence rules in this place were my new language-learning assignment. But until I became fluenter, I blurted and my speech was lapped up with relish. Blunt talk was a rare delicacy. It was speech caviar in that vicinity.

My village. Where I blew in, secured a place with light and a river view. Where I learned saying *hi* was de rigueur when meeting villagers in the byways. Where I liked living amidst great talkers even if I wasn't a great talker myself. I liked the murmur, the easy cheeriness. I marvelled then and still I marvel at their fluency. I liked being immersed in living talk, as if I were being supplied with a linguistic mustard plaster. Because I had been hurt by language's lack. Yes, it was a healing.

A langer said that there was a dare in The Crested Grebe. Grab the lifeless, leaden hairpiece that graced Mick Rhatigan's pate. The tale went that a drunk did get up the nerve, nabbed Mick's man-wig, ran and flung it in the back field. Naturally, he was lifetime Grebe-barred.

64

The first years were tea years. Any time, day, night, didn't matter, when a friend's fist rapped the glass, it was chat time. Bun time, digestive bickie time, hang-and-butter sandwich time, even I that didn't like tea made Barry's after Barry's with milk, never black. Fergal'd put half the sugar bag in. Us at the table, rain battering the glass, RTÉ blaring, cars splashing the puddles at the turn in the bridge, sheep baa-ing in the lane. Passing the time with tea and talk. Fergal chatted chatted. I straightened the place mat, aligned knife with napkin, turned milk jug perpendicular, crushed crumbs under my fingers, brushed them in little piles beside the little sugar crystal piles, silently measured which pile was higher, tasted them, pushed them under my fingernails, dug them free. Listened.

He said there were days when the entire village was in sync with a fire insurance scheme. Guys actually burned their farms deliberately and claimed the insurance. There was a schedule. Every farmer agreed which guy was burning which day and each guy's farm'd blaze and then they'd make the claim. Burn in Turn they called it. It persisted. Claims piled up until the Dublin insurance guys figured what was happening, started investigating and the scheme went defunct.

Then there was the German TV crew that came and filmed Fergal sticking a live flapping duck up the chimney in a damp place near Keadue. He claimed it was the best auld Irish cleaning way. Black wings. The cratur. He'd evilly laugh. It was anarchy, it was pure anarchy, he said, the way I like it. He said chimbley. He said he was frikend. He said, If I'd been educated I'd really be harmful. As it is, I'm just a muck savage. Then he'd leave because he said there was a little mystery needed investigating in Frenchpark and Fergal was just the man. In the early days I'd jump in the van, and he'd drive every bumpy lane, telling me the disappeared names and faces, when they emigrated and why. Then came the Germans and Dutch. They rescued the auld places that'd fallen in bits. They plastered and heated them, made them dry, dug the fields, planted spuds, cabbages, leeks, filled the quiet yards up with children's cries again. I think he liked them because it was like travelling. He'd rap their glass, plunk at their farm tables, hear the Dutch and German ways. He was interested in everything, big man-bear that he was. Hands like grizzly paws cupping the steaming mug heavy with sugar. I heard that back in the day when he was drinking, punters gave him wide berths because they knew he'd easily kill a man with the hands. Even if he wasn't meaning. As it was he wasn't drinking when I knew him. If he heard there was a man in Kerry that was in deep shit with the drink, Fergal'd jump in the van and drive Ireland. Help. Help was his way. He dug friends' graves. He scattered my steps with fresh cut greenery at Christmas. February first, St Brigid's Day, he'd scatter spring buds again at May Day. A great man in a crisis is what they said. It was true. He was true even with all the fibs he spun.

65

New Jersey behind me. New Jersey a fair few lifetimes away. Family in smithereens, the suburbs getting richer, Mafia-ed and reality TV-ed (*Real NJ Wives* was set there). Here was I in this wet, rural scene ruled by rain, cattle and ancient grudges. My new life was enabled by the Internet and easy travel away when I wanted. Emails and reading the web kept me feeling my past was still attached. My granny lacked such luxuries when she left Ireland a hundred years earlier. She left, was bereft. A thing I will never experience, yet a thing I sense in my waters.

The village was as unhurried as Mick Murphy's put-put farm vehicle, which he navigated at a snail's pace. Travelling leisurely let Mick take in every cattle feeder in wet fields, every new car with recent reg, every petunia in every new hanging basket placed by the Tidy Village Team. Eagle Eye he was, slumped at an angle against the sweaty plastic rain shield. Mick Murphy's sluggishness was legendary in Ireland. I met Munster guys that knew there was a farm vehicle in my village snails were faster than.

I'd buy bread and milk in Mary's and get what else I needed in SuperValu in Carrick. In winter, the vegetable display was cabbage displayed against cabbage leaves. In summer there were beets, spring cabbage, spuds and salad leaves reared under glass in Ballinaglera. Spaghetti was pasta. Beverages were tea, milk and Nescafé. Milk. Tap water was suspect. Fridays were steak and lamb-leg days getting Sunday-ready. Steak with chasseur sauce. Apple tart with cream. Breakfast sausages, eggs, black pudding, rashers, sliced pan.

Then came the Great Latte Shift. Circa 2006, caffè lattes became available in Mullingar, meaning the landscape had shifted permanently. Massive blueberry muffins, basmati rice packets, papayas, French baguettes, Vietnamese fish sauce, basil and chilli plants appeared. A new, gigantic SuperValu went up in the fields that were inundated every January by the winter rains that swelled the river. The planners didn't mind, it seemed. A cinema built beside the SuperValu was later swamped in winter high waters, the red velvet seats drenched. In every vacant field black-and-white planning flyers went up, stapled in sweaty plastic sleeves that leaked rain and became unreadable.

Standing at my kitchen sink, I watched diggers and trucks scrape flat the hill-cap beside the river, making building space. A luxury estate, with places with large plate-glass apertures went up there, named after a village in deep Sussex. Guards, nurses, insurance guys, start-up entrepreneurs purchased them. Urban-style estates sprang up like weeds in Carrick, in Keadue, even in Ballyfarfar. Latvians and Lithuanians immigrated in their numbers and signed up as hired hands at the building sites. Their delicacies began appearing in Lidl: unusually curled-up fish and icy, pale dumplings in plastic bags languished in freezers. Pimped-up cars driven by Lithuanians accumulated in car parks. Tall, clean-shaven, muscularly built men were seen lifting weights in public gyms far and wide, having incalculable impact. Native Irish hankered after the leggy, flaxen-haired girls that arrived. Riga, Gdansk, Vilnius became Irish family wedding settings and Ryanair quickly expanded their flight paths.

The estate agents' flyers hawked a rural lifestyle, but there wasn't anything rural in it. It was all cars, appliances, barbecues, timber decking, lifestyles. Rururbia a friend called it. Urban Farms had arrived in rural Ireland. A helipad was arranged as busy execs needed fast Dublin escapes, needed leisure and beer imbibement. Brand-new Mercedes sedans, their back seats ferrying bags filled with DIY materials, garden figurines, Leyland cypress hedging and pansy seedlings sped up hills, raced past wimpled auld ladies walking pushbikes with Denny's rashers, Brennans bread and Fairy liquid in their wire baskets. Time was shrinking. Tea and chats were getting squeezed by busy BlackBerry diaries. Then there was what digital piracy did. Hippies in yurts in Leitrim fields were binge-watching *The Wire* with subtitles. Cats named McNulty appeared and scampered near bins. Swing sets and jungle gyms appeared in gardens. Leisure became a thing. Pampas grass fucking everywhere.

It was happening fast in all the rural areas. We were in a stunned silence as the diggers, piled high with 'material' (aka earth) rumbled by. Then the dreaded black-and-white planning flyer appeared tacked up beside the triangular field in the village centre. Thirty-five semi-ds, an urban-style estate, was planned where cattle were currently munching. A man with a lucrative building equipment-rental business in the next parish had enlargement ideas. The Murphy family'd make a tidy sum selling the land. If each semi-d were priced at 350K, the takings were plenty bankable.

66

The lane behind the mail-delivering lady's place was where picking blackberries was best. Being tucked away, there wasn't any street dust, weedkiller and mutts with their dirty lifted back legs. The berries were clean, darkest and sweetest there, glistening ripe fly eyes in the hedges that we ate, sun-warm.

My time in the village is measured in the ditched cars that had been her mail delivery vehicles. The farther back in the lane, the farther back car-time – which is time – went. Blackberry-picking became a walk in a village archive. The blue VW Passat was still intact, parked up near the back wall. Then the silver Astra, missing a windshield and back tyres. Then the white Renault van, nearly unremembered, glass entirely absent, carrying trumpet vine, bindweed and brambles as passengers. Finally a twisted rusted thing missing paint, wheels, axles. Just a chassis, the make indiscernible. That was way way back in the day.

67

Mick Rhatigan's pitiable man-wig lying in the field behind The Crested Grebe, amidst sheep shits, thistles, nettles, turf briquette-chip detritus. See it in the rainy winter days when the sun barely exerts itself behind the dark pines, its real-hair-effect plasticized fibres tickled by the wind. His dull grey man-wig lying there every winter night, sheep stepping in it, rats, rabbits and badgers sniffing it then running after better quarry.

68

Sienese pigments in jars. Pestled very fine. Sienese pigments in jars lined up in my shelf:

jar jar jar jar jar.

Carried in U-Hauls and car trunks aways aways. Veneeshan Red, Burnt Umber, Raw Sienna, Yeller Earth and Tair Vairt. Rubbed between fingers hue spreads sticks makes visible waves fingerprint grain map. Such fineness. Like talc, like dust, like beremeal – the cake we'd make with these hues! Mix in water – pigment awnkmint. Paste.

Terra Umbra Bruciata manufactured by Ricci Belle Arti in Siena reads the label. *Terra per pittura.*

Sacred pigment because it generated fifteenth-century pictures that still instruct twenty-first-century me.

Rubbed in handskin I get a shade darker, umberer, less pink. If inhaled I might expire but I'd venture eating even if unpregnant.

Warmest hue! Italian hill guys dug up and pleasure-milled it. Pinkie plunged in jar-deep pigment, velvet umber clings, my hand is singular umbered expelled dignified: burnt.

Her hair had been auburn then it went champagne grey. *Like Katherine Hepburn,* my father always said with a wistful gleam in his blue eye. With my hand pigmented thus I draw her nearer. She's dead and buried years and years and years but this pigment crushes time, pigment I squeeze between my fingers, giving grief a hue that is burnt but reddish. I begin by painting her hair, its terrier texture, get in her vicinity and paint that missing space between us, it's warm and ablaze.

Her tweed suits, the smart jacket-and-skirt sets she packed in her suitcase after she'd paid a decent price in Dingle. She'd even tried haggling but it didn't fly. Treasures they were. She wrapped herself in fabrics garnered in her materfamilias' hunts in Ireland. I see them in the same hue as the dried turf we disbelieved was earth burnt in their Stanleys that kept the farm kitchen warm. Burning earth! That was barbaric and they were relatives! I see her, smell her in her tweed suit and crisp white shirt, the kind smirk she'd make when she gazed at me thinking I didn't see. But I saw. Terrier hair, tweed suit, buttery skin, smirk, material that was my mam but I never called her Mam. I see her, smell her, feel her but I can't hear her. I bet her timbre was like my aunt's with the Jersey-isms edited because better speech meant she might be educated, which she wanted, which she wasn't. Her speech has disappeared. Burnt up.

She wanted culture but she wasn't sure what culture was. She felt it. Museums felt like culture. Libraries. She ferried me as a girl there: museums and libraries in Italy, in France, in England. She released and relaxed her high-strung mind in them. She must have met herself there, reflected in bits, shattered and elusive but palpable in her depths. Meanwhile she was planting me. I was her seed, planted in Titian's thrashingly brushed underpainted surfaces, in Edgar Degas's warm grisaille self-regard, in Mary Cassatt's fantasy-daughters' dark eyes, in Dürer's hare's fur, the spiky white, auburn and black hairs.

Her mind, its acuity and wit stranded in an acre-subdivided suburb, pressing against the sage-green painted walls, nearly splintering the lapstraked white timber cladding, simmering in the slubby felted yarns braided in a circular rug in the den. That rug burbled with her leashed vitalities. I bear her, her intellectual hunger, her wit, her creative urges that dabbled in knitting, crewel arts, refinishing furniture, scrubbing everything. Crewel and scrubbing she was, straining straining straining, leaning but never getting anywhere she really wanted.

Where she eventually went: plummeting savagely inwards. Her mind, her hunger, her wit, her fierceness, her rage driven deep and dark in her viscera, festering.

Earth she has lain in these fifty years in New Jersey. Burnt Umber the expensive walnut casket she was placed in and kept shut in at the wake – wasted away with the cancer, she wasn't presentable. Her blue eyes, freckled hands, buttery skin, dark viscera, sturdy skeletal frame, terrier hair retaken by the New Jersey earth, that unvisited immigrant graveyard. Her remains, his remains – their remains: shipwrecked in that suburb. The placemat-sized granite markers endure freezing winters and scalding summers year after year after year, uncleaned, untended. What remains in me, carrying.

5
SHITE

69

While the Celtic Tiger was raging, I went travelling, getting a few respite weeks in Warsaw and parts east where capitalism was still a windy baby – nascent, fussing frequently, but still experiencing milk- and sleep-fed peaceful spells. A warm humid day in July, when the hedges were lush and The Crested Grebe's beer garden was wedged with Emerald Star cruiser crews, I returned. There was a tangerine JCB parked in the triangular field and a massive mucky gash in the earth where my septic field had been. Water puddled in it, its surface bearing an unpalatable greasy lustre. There was a gigantic clay hill beside the gash equal in measure with the crater where it had earlier resided and was called 'earth'. The ancient perimeter wall had been razed at the west side, presumably in facilitating JCB access. There was an ugly, deep graze in the retaining wall between my place and the street, where the JCB's bucket must have eagerly swung as it made its way field-ward.

A bigger-than-usual advertisement had been erected at the field's western apex. It was a blue, red and white number, advertising 45 luxury semi-detached dwellings called Badger Ridge. It said payments were currently being accepted. A river view with blue sky and full sun was depicted beneath the text. The sign faced the river and cars that entered the village via the bridge met the sign, which prevented their viewing the field, the church, the pubs either side, and the sky. The sign prevented my seeing the river and the sunset as well. The sign bullishly depicted the river with a perpetually blue sky. It was an exceedingly effective impediment, tall and braced with timber 2-by-4s.

The whispered speech in the village was reaching Peak Mutter.

Just wait. It'll all crash in a few years. These places will be empty. We didn't learn anything after what we seen in England and America. We Irish let the place be ruined. Cluttered [heavy Leitrim 'r']. *All packed in like tinned mackerel. The village is changed, smashed up, shattered. Where will they get these buyers?*

Because I wasn't native, I was a safer bet with their shared secrets as my allegiances were few and situated at a thin depth – any allegiances I might have had were certainly un-ancient. If I were heard speaking against Badger Ridge, I didn't risk upsetting family alliances that had been in place since the Famine. I gradually learned that direct speech in public made against Badger Ridge was a terrible risk in this village. I learned as well that many villagers wished I'd speak publicly in their place as I had less at stake. This was an issue.

70

A deep night in August, the village was velvety and silent. The birds, cattle and I were asleep. There were few cars, especially as it was midweek. The sky was an inky blue-black with just an amber tint in the east, which was the street lights in Carrick. Suddenly there were distinct thuds heard; I didn't fully startle and wake up, but I recalled the dull thuds when I awakened the next day. I pulled aside the curtains and there was my river. My true-blue river with the uninterrupted grey sky reflecting in it. A realer picture. The giant sign had disappeared. A saw had been wielded in the night. Quite skilfully as it happens – the cuts were clean and quickly achieved. The thing was felled, and it lay in a gravel ditch, with rebar, my raw sewage and mud. It was the single brazen act against Badger Ridge that I had as yet witnessed.

71

True silence is an interval, a space, a blessed rest within a restless gale. Ilya Kaminsky says that silence is invented by the hearing, that the deaf abjure silence.[22] Even if they are frequently elided in usage, *silence* isn't the same as *unspeaking*.

Unspeaking can be a malignancy.

I arrived in the village as an individual hurt by unspeaking, specifically Hers, which had impeded my ways with speech internally and externally as well.

> *I have been so dislanguaged by what happened*

as David Ferry puts it.[23]

Gab attracted me. I was awed by the way a villager might spend fifteen minutes telling a stranger that the weather hadn't yet exceeded summer 1996 when they had their tea in the garden every evening that June and July and swam in the river after as the heat was that withering. In New Jersey the summers were always steaming and New Jersey denizens spent little time in discussing it – did better weather engender clipped speech? That seemed simplistic, like mistaken essentialism, but I felt that by immersing myself in that gabby place I might be reinstated with a linguistic fluency that had been nearly extinguished in me. By what? By the suburbs, by the market, by death-denial, by whiteness, by the USA? I wasn't sure. But I had inklings.

'Having the chat' became my language rehab lab. I'd watch the pitch-and-catch pattern that set up between practised rural Irish chatterers. Neither held the chat 'ball' very much; it was always pitched back – that way the talk circulated and didn't stagnate. With finesse, they executed gymnastic verbal timings, witticisms, rare earnestness, much laughter. (I watched as Americans, including me, held the ball – thinking thinking thinking – as that scintillating chat energy leaked away.) Language was indeed a circuit, a game. It required at the very least a pair – that kept the chat aerated and alive. And language demanded time as well, giving and taking time.

Immersed in that chat lab I was listening listening listening. A speech urge might rise like an inner tide inside, but my larynx wasn't very supple. Language slid back in my gullet and sat there, weighty. I felt the backed-up talk accumulating in my flesh, hardening and thickening in my cells, a sticky plugged-up-ness. It felt like a cancer.

A particularly female cancer, as it happens, as many males are permitted speech at the start, are be-knighted with speech entitlements. Their speech rights are given at birth. They talk talk talk if they want. Many females struggle in reaching fluency, hesitating, feeling unentitled, checking their veracity against men's. What a lifetime it can take finding that speech right. First inside. Then translating that inside talk and making it external talk. It's hard graft, building that internal-external linkage then flinging language in a marketplace, a lecture hall, a farm gate, a village green, a piazza, a street. Yet it is a leavening.

Speech makes inner language public. Lips are the valve. When talk happens, an inner hiss is heard, there is a general easing, pressure releases. The flesh lightens. Language slips in listeners' ears and is then internal in the listener. Language is an exchange; it is isn't an individual's game. Transmit – receive – transmit – receive. Internal – external exchange. That is the fluvial way with language.

72

In the early twenty-first century my New Jersey firstplace became matchsticks. A digger razed it. Piled in dumpsters and hauled away, my family residence was chucked in a landfill in Pennsylvania. It had been built in 1963 – it wasn't ancient. The buyer's new architect specified a larger plan and a greater height – lake views, which added value – and a palace went up in its place. It was framed in ply that, when wet, resembled gingerbread. There is indeed a fairy tale undercurrent streaming in all the new places that have sprung up in Urban Farms since my family disintegrated. The residences appear as if they've ingested pills that have magicked atria, pillared arcades, marble vestibules, wisteria-laden archways, parquet-bricked driveways. A fairyland attained when the bank balance brims with cash.

Panzavecchia, Hrbek, Ruczewski, Dambruwski, Chatgachbanian, Magillicuddy, Klimczak, Ianucci, Kwiatkawski, all the strange names in the nearby graveyard.

The gap between the actual Urban Farms and my remembered experience creates a time-space dizziness. I remember the twists in the streets, the familiar angles, particular perspectives seen between trees that are fifty years past. A speed bump that hasn't changed at all. What was a dilapidated apple farm in my day is an exclusive club these days. I'm seeing everything thru wavy glass: buckled views here, clarified views there.

The Urban Farms denizens and their estates. Just say a family name and in an instant there is the full grasp, the feeling, the package, what they were, what my parents had said, tales that lingered because they had believability. A hue, a density, a smell these inhabitants emitted: the guy with the gauze taped where his ear had been. He was missing a digit as well – a lawn-cutting accident is what was said. His wife in a Hawaiian muumuu always. A vague, sinister undercurrent in the parents that fruited in addict children and dramas. There was the French man that raved at the TV dinners' tastiness served up when he arrived in his Firebird chez Prideaux at half past five each weekday evening. His wife had lingered at the tennis club until five, raced back in the Cadillac and heated up the dinners with lightning speed. These tales are all packed densely in the site where they were in the district, their single-acre identities. Tale after tale after tale after tale after tale. The narratives lined up in leafy, tribally named streets.

73

It starts when the gall wasp crawls beneath a tree leaf and lays its eggs in a puncture in the leaf's structure. As the larvae mature, the tree secretes tannic and gallic acids, and an awkward ball appears in the leaf structure. A gall. When the larva matures, it escapes the gall and leaves a little puncture. That little wasp begins and leaves via piercing and interrupting the leaf structure. Fly away little wasp, fly!

The ugly gall that remains in the leaf is a chief ingredient in writing- and drawing-ink. The galls are picked, dried, pestled, then mixed with water. Vinegar can be used with the same end result. The element Fe, when put in sulfuric acid, yields Fe sulphate, a fine, dusty, greenish residue. When Fe sulphate is mixed with the tannic acid in wet, pestled galls, it creates, via chemical synergy, a very dark material, a pigment: an ink – gall ink. Acacia trees yield a sap, which when harvested and dried is called gum arabic. Mixed with a little water, gum arabic can put brilliance and thickness and stability in gall ink.

When the gash appeared in the triangular field, when the shit started backing up in the septic tank, when the massive earth pile equal in size with the rent earth just sat there muckily, when the nervy letter appeared saying my septic system had been linked with the new village system and if I'd simply sign away any rights … when the builder's men in the field whispered it was a buncha bull and never never sign, when the next letter arrived claiming there wasn't any septic field in the field's deed, when the legal phrases, tight and chilly, began being bandied, when the builders secured lawyers and when lawyers were secured by me in reply, when the farmer appeared weekly with the pipe that emptied the backed-up shite and filled his tanker truck, when he sprayed the shit in faraway fields, when the luxury places multiplied and engulfed the village's sweetness, when Lehman became a widely said name in rural Ireland, when the half-built estates became windswept rat, bat, slug and snail sanctuaries, when bitterness invaded the veins as we were swept up in a rising debt tidal wave that swamped us and caused debt fist fights excessive drinking pill-taking bankruptcy mayhem emigratings suicide murder and a widespread unravelling, when all the rain that fell in the triangular field trickled in the dank gash, trickled beneath the street and travelled up, up, up, filling my septic tank cemented at the gable wall, mixing with my daily sewage, causing a crisis, when there wasn't any shite egress and it threatened backing up inside the WC, when the tanker was being filled and the pipe went berserk, spraying the farmer's jumpsuit with raw sewage, when I perceived deep panic in the farmer's eyes at the spattered shite, the diseases it bred, and I averted my eyes as he shed the dirtied blue jumpsuit and shit-stained wellies and dressed in the ancient tweed suit and cap that were in the van, when the letters N–A–M–A were magicked in a new sequence with a new meaning and a cement truck, churning, with the hand-painted failed bank's name spinning dizzily was driven at the State's central gates by a spalpeen, when the black black shit backed up in an entire state, when it all hit the fan, then gall ink – its inherent, dark and sundry might as an inquisitive instrument, a digger-upper, a wakey-up tincture, a balm prescribed when gaping debt and multiplying minus signs caused bleeding by a hundred St Sebastian cuts – its usefulness as an incendiary self- and civic-investigative medium asserted itself, did gall ink.

When humans shifted language fundamentally, grabbed it in the air and flung it earthward at their level and infused a material with it, they made speech appear in paper. Gall ink was the substance that made this widely happen. Gall ink is a carrier. When gall ink hits paper it gets blacker and blacker. It fetches revenge, bitterness, shite, anger, sublime states as well: happiness, pleasure, lust – these bind with the vellum-paper's surface and vibrate. Vital fluids leach away and are altered in the vellum-paper's fibres in the writerartisting act.

74

When the village went septic, when rural renewal had made it an Urban Farm, I went septic myself. Blind in my eyes and in my feelings, I knew I was enraged but I didn't have a clue at what. A skewed lad had made a sign that said DEVILIPERS and marched with it as if the dudes with the land, diggers and cash had been devils – and it was true they had been dirty dealers – but they weren't instigating things. Implicated, yes, yet they were pawns as well. The culprit was larger and diffuser, was invisible and mighty, like the Bible's Guy in the Sky if that Guy in the Sky were practised in usury. Where was it? What might I rant at, what might I fight? I was blind and wanted sight. I feared I'd crumble inward, rage like Ezra P. did at usury, but misguidedly, aimlessly, diffusely. I needed perspective and distance, yet I was immersed and enswamped. Where might my rage be aimed?

Film, being a seeing medium and a material that might capture reality and give perspective, might give a clue, I mulled. I hired a massive reflecting surface – thing was as big as a king-size mattress – rigged it standing up in a trailer, clamped a 16 mm film camera there, aimed it half at the glass and half at the 'real' scene, and cruised the streets. A Latvian friend manned my VW diesel pulling a trailer. There was a deep January freeze and river mist gripped the village hard. The film trapped the unwinding scenes in split screen. Pebble-dashed dwellings, drenched fields, lichen-flecked walls, winter hedges, beech trees, the pebble-dashed church, the pubs, a guy in high-vis gear, a kid-gang, gripping crisp bags and waving at us – all were filmed as half-actual and half-reflected. The ugly, half-built estates were mist-scrimmed and mystery-filled in that weather – bettered. At dusk everything went purple and the sulphur street lights made blurry, citrus-hued spheres that scattered and diffused amber light in driplets as if Seurat were painting the village. Heartbreaking in its beauty and its strange, skewed splitness, the film is a relic I will keep, a life-in-the-village remnant, a priceless lifetime trapped in amber.

Yet the filming was a failure as a distancing, critical lens with which I might see and understand what had happened. Summing up wasn't within my reach. I erred, perhaps, if I weigh up what I captured, in gathering a certain thing even when I wasn't aiming at it. Beauty jumped in that Latvian-driven trailer, in that massive reflective glass, in the camera lens. Beauty flirted with and French-kissed the sensitive 16 mm film deep in the camera and beauty tickled the megapixels in the sensing machine in the DSLR until it gave up and let itself be utterly seduced. I didn't want it; I spurned it and turned away yet beauty kept at me and the hired cameras.

A single scene that lifted beauty's hem and went beneath it: I'd directed the driver that he pass with the glass in the trailer, again and again, by the distinctively tall sign advertising the new estates. It was a high, rectangular affair, rigged with 2-by-4 stilts like an elevated pulpit with Badger Ridge in serifed lettering and the estate agent's name and website in Helvetica. We fixed the film camera's lens at an ancient, hand-built wall with a Leyland cypress hedge behind and a steel grey sky in the frame's upper half. As the glass-in-trailer passed by in the viewfinder, the tall estate agent's sign appears and disappears as the trailer exits the frame stage left. We did many takes at different speeds, and edited them in a sequence that animates the sign, making it a spectral presence appearing in the sky, interrupting the hedge, and then vanishing.

Maybe it helped place the activity in a larger time frame, that the land and the hedges and the sky at least might remain after the market had pillaged the place like an avenging angel.

Single thing that camera delicately articulated in that generally failed film experiment: the market mightn't gulp everything.

75

Filmic treatments began suggesting themselves.

1. The Digger and the Church: a massive earth heap has been piled up with a JCB sitting at the peak. The high-vis tangerine digger is acidic against the rare blue summer sky. Using animated text placed directly in the landscape, the sequence underlines the day when the digger became higher than the church, the day the market had surpassed the church as the village's highest value.

2. Archival Interlude: 8 mm film intercuts, depicting Leitrim in the early 1970s (in film-maker's family archive). Village residents narrate the sequence.

3. The River as Amphitheatre: the camera is trained at the river with the building sites in the distance. We hear rhythmic hammer taps reverberate in the space between the river and the sky. Their music carries the segment.

4. Viewfinder: *In the shed beside the barracks / in the shaded February damp / I feel I am standing in a camera / The shed walls frame a picture / the river and the riverbank / sunlit luxury dwellings / all lined up facing The View.* The text is placed in a shed beside the barracks where McGahern grew up, and the camera pans the text and landscape: the dilapidated shed, the barracks, the river, the new, empty luxury estates at the river, which face the barracks.

5. *Launch!*: an animated fantasia in which a river cruiser trailing a waterskier navigates the empty estates.

6. Funeral Beauty: a large funeral re-enactment. Many dress in high-vis vests and direct cars as they traverse the bridge.

7. Building Site Pas de Deux: vignette featuring high-vis vests. Male ballet dancers dressed as hired hands stir sand and wiggle beside a cement mixer.

8. The Reliable Squeak in the Gate: lyrical segment featuring a squeaky gate via which villagers can visit The Crested Grebe.

9. Cabbage White Flitter: the cabbage white butterfly is tracked by the camera as it visits the weedy and cultivated patches, the rusting rebar, bath tile shards, PVC piping and spilled cement, in the disturbed triangular area.

76

Ink, film, pigments, graphite, a typewriter and an inkjet printer were media that mattered much after my place and the village itself were wrecked by the new estates. My public speech was inept. September 2008 the RTÉ guy with the mic appeared and asked things, thinking he had a live wire here. (My letters in the newspapers, attempts in fluency, signalled this.) But with that fuzzy mic at my chin, I was seized by nuance and enigma. Try as I might, I failed at finding summative statements. I hated what had happened in that village, but I knew that Rhatigan wasn't really the devil incarnate as the gravedigger had maintained, that the digger/builder guy was already suicidal, and what was gained by vibrating my larynx and enlarging this shrillness? The inquisitive fire in the RTÉ guy's eyes dampened as I sketched grey shades, my speech an awkwardly achieved grisaille palette that, when duplicated in his machine, became an indefinite mist – as if I had written a tract in graphite and hastily erased it. He'd travelled far. He had a deadline. Staff in Dublin were waiting. It was sad.

Yet speech in public places is tricky. True, it is an airing and a clearing away and there had been much unspeaking, much fetid held-back speech. Bravery is required in public speech-making yet it isn't bravery that always speaks. Dubravka Ugrešić says it is fast-talking that the cameras, the feeds, the mediathings want.[24] They want language heads. They want thinking in instants, making statements and facts that seem right in increment time frag-ments. These talkers and their events are seductive. In public talks, writerartists get arranged in upstage chairs (things) talking with a chair (human), purple gel lights rinsing them purple and the audience is rapt, hungry. I have been in that audience and in the twin chairs. Yet I query myself. What did Yeats call it, the smiling public man? Few are they that can live that. If pushed, I side with the stutterers, with the shy. Fanny asks (in paraphrase): what is a writerartist but a human that lives, that laughs, that listens / lacking pretence, understanding zilch / driven by the lyric's quest that never (G willing) will be divulged?

77

Try seeing the village. It mists up. Rub it away. Try again. Squint in the vagueness. Clarity in a split minute then it mists up again. Maybe a skewed angle will reveal, try it via the pets.

1. Dram Quigley: Lab with a bad limp. Free-range mutt. Ate anything dumped near any kitchen. Big shitter.

2. Chester Higgins: small and irascible Jack Russell Terrier: JRT. Chased cars with squat little legs swiftly sprinting. Never was hit. Clever. Curled up beside fires.

3. The Dimwits: innumerable and numberless. Black in a pack. Very dumb. Hunting spaniel ancestry but very few canny genes left. Incessant barkers. Always wet. Human family in a trad band.

4. Scud: diminutive, black-and-white sheep herder with brunette facial markings. Matted, bad-smelling in areas. Gentle, reliable. Graceful runner and fluid wall-jumper, bit like a pine marten. Ear-splitting barker. Upper lip bared in a genuine smile at friends' arrival. Excellent canine.

5. Rusty Puff at Leash-End: walked with lady that manned an upmarket dress place in Ballaghadereen. Fluffy. Diamanté lead, painted nails. Silent, puffy, resentful aspect.

6. Cattle Cat: white cat with large black patches like a Friesian. Ears utterly chewed away by incessant street fighting. Dirty. Scrappy. Skulker.

7. Champ: Rudiger's (the guy at the Riverside Restaurant, which all call Rudiger's). Large black-and-white farm mutt. Vague and unimaginative. Unclean, matted, shitty fur beneath tail always. Ball-bedevilled, ceaseless fetcher. Harmless but might turn, I feel.

78

Sienese pigments in five jars that travelled the earth with me but I hadn't a clue in what ways they'd be handy. That they were beautiful was a given and I have held them many times in their jars and simply admired their gentility, the quiet hue-leaps they make: yeller – Sienna – umber – earth red – earth green. Never big jumps. It is their subtle, deliberate, reticent shifts in hue, their character and quality that impress me.

These hues always stir the imbibement urge, but death might result, and I resist. It may be the case that I will paint a still life that includes these pigment jars and a black Braun travel timepiece I particularly admire. It has a black black case, a circular face and white numerals, white hands with a thin yeller needle that marks each small time increment with a jerk and a tick. I like it beside the yeller pigment jar with the white lid capturing chilly Irish light. All these elements chiming nicely: the white, the yellers and mustards, the deep black against the rich flaxen-jarred pigment. Like Cézanne's early still lifes it is a fine scene yet the image isn't the urge. Yes, I might set up a palette and splurge it with pigment pastes, arrange a brush spray, filberts and brights, bunched in a tall tin can, decant turpentine in a jam jar, linseed in a lid, and begin. I might. But it is the pigment itself, its factness that snares me. That humans searched tints in the landscape, dug them up, humped them, classified, pestled, packaged, shipped them and artists figured what they'd make with them. It's the pigments themselves I'm after.

Mustard shag carpet, my inner speech stuffed in that teen chamber all these years. Muffled, captive, driven inward and inaccessible. A speech bubble levitating near me, travelling everywhere with me, always that feeling that there were things I felt, things I knew, things that had happened that were real yet buried, that wanted saying. That bubble's presence was near, mustard-hued, visceral like puke yet valuable like a priceless metal. Durable. The messy task, time-drenched, as the speech bubble breaks asunder, in small pinpricks, in sideways swipes, in spaces when it's least expected. My life since in sum.

In a quiet, half-ugly/half-glam shade like margarine, like failed wedding rings, like bile, like a sky in a gale, maybe the day after a hurricane, early, when the land is picked clean and built things are thrashed, when the light has a scrubbed feel, the yeller-pigmented telling tells. That unreachable speech lets fly, ventures an utterance, sees if its intimate is in a listening stance. Unbidden, it is a bewilderment.

79

His fingers are pudgy. They grip the filter's black handle, which is warm and shaped by his hand and the innumerable times he has wielded it. He flicks the switch, and the bean-grinding machine gives a grating metallic whirr, which he simply disregards. The blare just isn't admitted in his sensual apparatus. Tim hears Deep Purple, the wailing guitar licks, and screeching Metallica in the excellent Kef speakers all right, but the grinder's irritating whirr? This barista isn't taking it in.

He pulls the grinder lever twice and releases fragrant, pulverized, nearly burnt beans in the right measure in the filter's basket. Then he picks up the weighty silver tamper, presses and twists it until the puck is flattened and level. Gingerly, he runs his third finger's fingertip in the filter's metal bevel and traces a circle, gathering stray java particles that might interfere with the gasket's seal and the steam pressure. Unthinkingly, he flicks them away. With an accurate, practised gesture, he swivels the filter up and secures it in the massive Gaggia. Tim flips the brew switch and flicks it again by feel when he's sure the caramel-hued crema is fully manifest in the little glass that catches the syrupy liquid.

All the while Tim is talking – telling me the live sketch he saw last night, which was excellent in places, like the Flying Circus in their best days, but updated and funny in an Irish way. His lengthy hair is thick, brushed aside and slung behind an ear. It's dark, similar in hue with the beverage he serves, but here and there a wiry, stray grey hair like a busted guitar string sticks up.

I have watched Tim palm his skull and flatten these hairs when he's having a cigarette break, while he gazes at the cars in the car park, the measly grassy area with the dried-up animal turds, the sizeable beech tree and the rusting street furniture with all his regulars' dirty cups and ashtrays piled up. His café fills up at breakfast and after lunch, and I have never seen Tim ruffled by the queues, by impatient business types, by the special vegan and American iced beverage requests, by the latte versus flat white explainings. He takes his time and he visits with his clients. He pitched this small café in the Celtic Tiger's excrement as an expectant gesture in a dark time. He built a relaxed gathering place and within it, Tim is relaxed: the het-up citizens can get fleeced and their fast fucking java at Starbucks.

The dark Peruvian, Kenyan, Ugandan and Brazilian beans that arrive in burlap sacks trucked up by the Hungarian caffeine fiend based in Dublin are Tim's material and his element. Having spent his day grinding and steaming these beans, Tim is surely fragranced with them. I imagine his wife smiling at his familiar java-and-cigarette smell as she nestles in with Tim, telly-ready, after his day in the café.

80

I fear that She is still in an unsettled place, unresting. She just slipped away during a Wednesday in New Jersey, Her remains claimed and cleaned by the funeral men. There had been a wake in the funeral business premises, Her casket shut. I remember very little, the upheaval – Her death – caused my vanishing. Apparently I practised cheerleading with my friends in the hallways.

I wasn't there.

I am still in an unsettled place, unresting.

She wasn't an earthly creature. Slight, nervy, with a crackling wit, raging and fury-filled at times, She was lightning-like, She was placed in the sky, a *speir bhean* they'd call Her in Irish. Yet I feel She wants waked and buried, rightly. Truer perhaps, I need Her waked and buried that I might settle.

I see a table burdened with stews and sandwiches. The crinkled aluminium paper wrapping the dishes effuses a splintered, blinding metal glare, as it reflects and refracts the bright bulb in the kitchen's pendant lamp. The kitchen is filled with a steady murmur caused by human speech; many are speaking, laughing in raised pitches and whispering in hushed pitches. The hum's frequency swells and thins like a beating heart muscle. It plucks a grieving girl's sternum and bends it in a human wavelength. The music it makes with her is sad, impartial and distant. She feels its elsewhereness, its great scale. Elegies are like this; they start in a shared place and split in single threads that needle hearts, pierce them utterly yet there is a fastening in that needling, stitching music.

The girl walks in between the speaking beings. Their speech is an animated blanket in the higher air. She parts the draughts as she navigates. Their speech falls like drizzle and wets her.

In the den there is a casket and She is in it, dead and vulnerable. In the wake's hustle-bustle, Her family and friends and Her child, me, traipse by it as we'd traipse by a bench, carrying biscuit trays, empty mugs, rain gear that needs hanging up. A child's tiny metal car, which he and an uncle are messing with, brazenly drives beneath the casket table. Sheepish, the child creeps under, snatches the car and hightails it.

There are intended visits with the departed, as well, when an aunt might kneel, pray and perhaps pet her sister-in-law's freckled knuckles knitted with prayer beads. Is Her hand stiff and chilled? A daughter might chance finding the answer, kneel and venture reaching her hand in that space. Try Her cheekskin's feel. Meet Her deadness and be jarred by it. Pay tribute and thank via the flesh.

A scene she mightily spurns yet wishes she had had.

81

Where the turf is stacked, near the FUCK THE EU garden, in the puddles where the sky is trapped and shimmers, where the fluffy white seed heads burst and cast themselves widely.

It's quiet.

Illegal dumpers in summer are scarce. Their fridges, miserable and akilter, have been rusting in ditches leaking chemicals since midwinter and sit silently accusing. Hikers with their field guides aren't here; their trails are mainly nearer the sea.

The field is impressively landscaped with the fat Burnt Umber bars made by the mechanically extruded turf. They are like massive Kit Kats strewn in a tantrum by a giant child. Fertilizer bags packed with cut and dried turf interrupt the rectangular bars at intervals. In the breezes, alder leaves shudder and blink green – grey – green – grey, indicating rain. Slender birch trunks draw distant verticals, sky-white. Dried heather tufts are islanded in recent rain runnels.

Beneath drizzle, rain and heather, the earth is a steady substance. It has a specific gravity, a quality that invites, has invited me. Allmylife. Friable and tangible, it's a place I inhabit with my flesh and with my mind, a craved darkness. A refreshment.

When life is thin, when I am eked pale, my skin like beaten linen, it is that crumbly clay that I pack myself in. Its dark is darker than shut eyes, darker than a grave. Place where I die and re-ignite in the quiet and dank, flashing madder like a beet in rich earth.

82

March is the freezing-est. All winter the icy sea sits there getting frigider and frigider. My big adult dream was sea-swimming. In deep. Saw the triathletes with their triangular arms in a splashy pack way far away in the sea. Kicking up white water plashy plashy. Fun in numbers. Team players. And safer.

Signed up. Hiked the kinky rubber wetsuit up my squishy thighs. High-vis red swim cap like an eraser at the black pencil-me tip. Zip zip up the back. Vaselined my neck. Run in with the pack, screaming. Icy water scalds my bare ankles, bare feet. Burning acetylene sea making my feet lifeless appendages in minutes. But the salt smell is like a salve. Deepest freshest thing. First full dunk underwater and breath is scarce. Lungs seize in the freeze. Faster half breaths. Huh huh huh huh little breaths. Keep swimming, churning. Kick, kick, kick. Can't be still. Else.

Head under water. Sea-green dream churn. Freshest deep deep substance. Transparent. Spy dark seaweed scraps in the sand ten metres under. A few shells, little else. 'Sligeach' in Irish means 'shelly'. A watery desert here, sunken. Land dwellers are unaware.

I'm swimming in this desert's sky. Green water-air, icy friend that hurts. My face is freezing, getting rubbery. Brain is fruz, aching. Paralysed lungs. This is crazy. Why? All us swimmers think thus in single heads. But the pack keeps Australian crawling, angling at the first marker, fifty metres away. Friends splashing either side. Leader Sheena, paddling a kayak, yelling: swim swim swim! We reach the painty metal ball, tread water, checking faces, blue lips, stiff, reddened skin.

But ah, bright eyes! Half-fear, half-bliss in the water say the eyes.

All here? All alive? screams Sheena. Then swim back! Quick, like!

Swim like the devil. Breakers carry us the final twenty metres. Then the strand under green, pleated Ben Bulben. Navigating slippery shingle. My feet are stiff ice shards. Can't feel. Can't slip in flip-flips. Fumble. Fuck it, just grab the flips, run up the beach, up the stairs. Each swimmer has a car-cum-changing area. Trunk lid up and peel wetsuits like fruit skins, pesky fruit skins. Chuck them in tubs. Warm wrap-ups. Mugs steaming with tea. Biscuits. Milling, laughing, teasing apart the last twenty minutes in that sea. Next time, it'll be thirty. Next time, it'll be less freezing. Right? Maybe. Sure it will be.

Fight, flight, freeze when faced with dangers. I fruz. Thawing, I surprisingly find, is happening in this icy sea, awakening me. Bravery I didn't think I had. Swimming shakes up desire, laid in, layered in me like salted silvery fish in ice. My desire. Wiggling, shimmying, wanting, caressing, painting skin with my paintbrush fingers, feeling, fucking, kissing, thrusting, thrashing, swaying, licking, screaming. The sea is my bed. Breaking up ice, waking me up, fighting, unsticking, retrieving pieces I'd marked as dead. The sea is my bigger than me. The sea retrieves my bulk, the sea argues with smallness. Challenges it. In fact, washes it the fuck away.

Chinks at first. Beauty drew me. Signalling. Misht beauty rain beauty river beauty Ben Bulben beauty green beauty grey beauty rain rain rain beauty Sliabh an Iarainn beauty strand beauty wind beauty river river river river beauty fuchsia beauty blackberry beauty cairn beauty Arigna beauty speech beauty hare beauty Leitrim accent beauty whin bush beauty sky beauty sun-lack beauty talk beauty lie beauty big fucking yarn beauty

beauty lace curtain beauty ass beauty sheep beauty cattle beauty beauty beauty head-the-ball beauty river cruiser beauty willie wagtail beauty birch alder beech beauty turf stack beauty talk talk beauty rippling river water in wind beauty hearty evil laughter beauty mink hunter beauty milky tea beauty anarchy beauty hazel beauty skinny deaf farm cat beauty pub quiz beauty Sheebeg beauty Derrygirraun beauty nettle beauty get-the-guards beauty silage bale beauty digger beside the church beauty scrap metal beauty dead and used-up animal truck beauty badger beauty new clean car beauty Cleaheen arched bridge beauty late-night chipper fight beauty fiddle flute guitar beauty air beauty grandchild-grandfather music playing beauty J. Meehan RIP's face beauty Rhatigan's squeaky gate beauty begrudgery beauty lingerie business in the Crash beauty sliveen beauty plamás beauty grá beauty Packie Duignan's flute beauty late night music in the pub beauty fer fuck's sake beauty fire in the grate beauty turf briquette beauty rarely seen stars beauty apples in the river beauty sewage beauty Leyland cypress beauty fucking hated pampas grass beauty sexless ageing female quilted-armless-zipped-garment-wearing beauty Inishmurray Inishmurray Inishmurray beauty beauty beauty Viking raid beauty car tax beauty crested grebe beauty unpaid TV licence beauty funeral beauty mass traffic jam beauty gay priest beauty champ beauty McCambridge's bread beauty hanging basket beauty Keadue Tidy beauty hedges beauty beauty guards busting drug-selling hippies beauty taking the piss beauty having a laugh beauty what's the craic beauty mighty beauty cuppa beauty late night kisses in the street beauty barge party beauty drunken banshee beauty turf fire in the pub beauty mineral beauty apple tart and fresh cream beauty sheep nuts beauty mart beauty lashing rain beauty I let the fruz sea beauty in and it blew my fruz in smithereens beauty.

6

CLASHYBEG

83

A gift came in the mail carefully wrapped with card, felt, newspaper and bubble wrap: a sandglass. A cherished Irish friend in Scandinavia purchased it in Hay. It arrived via a mailman's hands with a letter saying *here is a writing machine.*

Hand-made glass, transparent blue and amber, with twin tear-shaped chambers, like an inflated figure eight. When I upend it, the sand inside trickles and takes thirty minutes in its passing. Time elapses in the tiny, cinched sandglass waist. Pinched time, slipping between blue and amber chambers. The sand falls in tree-ring patterns in the amber base. Mica flecks in the granules glint like minute stars in my study's lamplight. Time piles up in the sandglass and when thirty minutes is up, a sand breast has been shaped with a dimple nipple in its centre. I upend the sandglass again, and amber-hued sand falls and fills up the blue chamber. Blue – amber – amber – blue, time's changing hues in the writing study.

First thing ever written by teenage me (that I remember) in the mustard shag place:

Sand Grain

Perceive me, pink-hued, in the small time granted as the sea will wash me away, take me elsewhere.

There had been a severance. There were many years living in bad faith with this WHAT these days I CALL MYSELF. Much blue-amber time elapsed when WHAT I CALL MYSELF wasn't palpable, was submerged in a different timeframe.

Feel. Latin: *palpus, palpare*.

It wasn't as if there wasn't anything in my head. There was plenty thinking. Sentences piled up in there and eddied infinitely. I put them in my diary, the sentences, the endless sentences. At least they made a fascinating pattern, what with my pleasant handwriting.

The blue sand grains are sliding and turning amber. Piling up. They make a faint, rustling whisper as they fall.

Whisper. Latin: *susurrus, susurrare*.

Whisper is the way it entered me this WHAT I CALL MYSELF. There was a teeny tiny little vent and it seeped in gradually and in time, disturbed the endless sentences that streamed in me, rustled beneath them as fresh autumn air lifts the leaves in a leaf pile and gently rearranges them. This thing WHAT I CALL MYSELF, I sensed it then it slipped away then came back. It seems that earthly materials are placed here as devices that enable WHAT I CALL MYSELF in sensing itself. In feeling the materials, I was palping me. Little by little in bits that I didn't think were anything because they felt like fragments. It felt like I wasn't an entirety and still feels thus.

Fragment. Latin: *fragmentum, fragere*, break.

Piece bit shard splinter particle speck chip sliver shaving paring snippet scrap flake shred tatter shiver spillikin smattering extract part chapter.

The sandglass, my writing machine, assists in my feeling time in the *minute*. *Minute* meaning a time unit and, as well, an infinitesimally small, whispered piece. The return, the path back, the re-fastening what had been severed has been in the *palp* and the *minute*. The trick: grab these divergent tracks, pull them, shape them. Make a single line. A pulse, a frequency.

Imagine the diviner's stick, a Y-shaped thing. *Palp* and *minute* make up the divergent lines in the Y. Grab the pair in each hand, exert pressure. Then they merge, the *palp* and the *minute*, they shape a single line, an *I*.

The I strikes the water where WHAT I CALL MYSELF lies, quivering.

The sandglass instructs me as I gaze at the grains traversing the needle's eye, the cinched waist where sand specks (the tiniest palps) are material and minute at the same time. Palp – minute – palp – minute – palp – minute – palp – minute.

Blue – amber – amber – blue – blue – amber – amber – blue.

That I can feel: a daily miracle.

In the feeling I discern this thing, this WHAT I CALL MYSELF and her/my weathers. Myself intrigues me, the way I transmute and am never very steady. Yet I find stability in the changes within this field WHAT I CALL MYSELF. I am the field in which things yearn and eschew. My pleasures, cravings and distastes shift and are peculiarly particular as if I'm in an unending pregnancy infinitely delivering myself: turf fires, bicycle rides, fenugreek cheese last week, this week ranunculus and freezing sea swims, next week perhaps early nights, music in earbuds and tea in bed with just me. Perhaps uhhn-uhn. Perhaps an unanticipated thing. What matters is that there are pleasures and distastes and they are in this felt field.

I relax in shelter and space, which is time where the market isn't yet king, where the gift is, and set the sandglass in the sill with Maeve's hill behind it. Maeve's alp helps me palp the days. When I raise my eyes up, see her heap where Maeve fierce queen, dead legend, is buried, I remember my life is larger than the smallness I am mired in.

Adjacency is grave.

My need is living in grave-adjacency with Maeve's cairn, that gravid bump, and all the dead stuff near and in sight. Maeve's cairn is my real timepiece. She clicks. I hear this best and clearly in the Sandy Field.

I use the sandglass as a spyglass and view Maeve's gravid grave largely while sitting at my desk.

Maeve's alp with her heap at the pinnacle. With signs all the way up saying RESPECT THE CAIRN'S SANCTITY. Circling the grave are signs planted in the clay depicting a figure climbing a cairn with a red circle and a line traversing it meaning CLIMBING UNLAWFUL, yet every time I'm up there kids are tramping up it and I yell at them saying can't they read the signs? Yes, I am that crank.

The knife-slice in a leaden sky at Strandhill that permitted a single sun ray, illuminated a lime green hillside when all else was grey in a day.

The sea's inimitable taste when first diving in and gulping it.

The cynicism that dwelt deep in me and has departed.

The space it left.

That I have lived in this west edge place near the sea in a space the market hasn't entirely captured.

84

Urban Farms wasn't a writerartist Petri dish; cash rather than culture was the gluey medium we were immersed in. With famine, ethnic cleansings, wars, and bank runs in immediate familial experience, survival and financial stability were desired and instilled in us. An artist's life and its precarities must be nipped in the bud if it raised its ugly head – it was a parent's duty. In Urban Farms, art wasn't a life path; art was aligned with lighting, tiles, carpets and panelling – a design issue. *What best matched the furniture?* was the pressing art inquiry in that paradigm.

My intense daily art-viewing experience back then was with a framed print, Seurat's *A Sunday at La Grande Jatte*, that hung in the WC beside the kitchen. Inside my head in the internal audible unit (I never heard/said the title in speech), I called it *La Grand Jat* (in a wide, internal New Jersey accent), and I gazed at it as my intestines emptied in the bleachy water beneath where I sat. Indeed, my daily WC visits and the aimless daydreaming permitted me there were tiny snicks in the facade I maintained, a facade in which I pretended that 'regular' family life was as interesting as when I was watching TV, reading and painting.

Seurat's idyllic lakeside scene with its distant sandy beach, the triangular white sails sailing and the bathers and picnickers beneath tall trees was very like the Indian Trail Club and the lake we swam in all summer. The dappled light was the same light as mine and New Jersey's – blue green in the shade and lime green in sun. But the large awkward bustles, the pencil skirts and tight-waisted jackets, the men's carefully barbered facial hair, their dapper high silk hats, canes and sun umbrellas were strange, delightful and alien – a relief, testament that life might be lived differently than in the bland place where I had landed. The little leashed capuchin with the curlicue tail, creeping beside a bustled, umbrella-ed lady, fascinated me. Where were capuchins kept as pets? The characters were drawn as calm, timeless statues, united in their half-lidded gazes, which were sludgy, dreamy and levelled at the lake. I admired the spatial rhythms they made in Seurat's careful arrangement. That a lucid thing might be made with small, vividly hued fragments was intriguing. I filed that away in the brain's deep creative unit.

Seurat's print lived in that pine-panelled WC, it hung there bearing its succulent fruit with an equally unlikely, shitting viewer. It fed my nascent painter's mind and my hungry eyes nearly a century after its making. But Seurat the human being, the painting's maker – where was he, I mused, and what enabled an artist's life?

The first thing I learned in the suburb is that art must sell. If sales weren't happening, then the art didn't have any value. I assumed that Seurat must have been successful and had many sales in his lifetime since here was his painting's image, matted in linen and framed in bevelled and metallic-leafed timber, in my Urban Farms WC. Same with Vincent V.G. His prints were everywhere – even in my art class, a girl was painting *The Starry Night*. Vincent V.G. must have hit the big-time sales, was the painting pinnacle, I inferred. Later I learned the real, sad Vincent V.G. life narrative, his mental anguish and deprived life and the degraded end in a French field. I saw that sales and success weren't a simple cause-and-effect thing, that there was a yawning gap between Vincent V.G. and *a* Vincent V.G.

With this cash-equals-success calculus firmly embedded in my psyche, there was set up a fundamental clash in me: while my artistic talent was being nurtured, its dedicated pursuit, as a calling and a career, wasn't, because there weren't any precedents. My relatives had been, as far back as we knew, farmers and servants, barkeeps and tradesmen with a single irregularity: Uncle Walter. My maternal uncle, her elder sibling Deaf Walter, was an artist all right, but at the first chance he skedaddled, ran away west, wrestled steers and made his living as a sign painter. I never met him. The single trace he left behind was a deft drawing in his little sister's diary: a Western rider and his prancing steed. The lyrical lines in blue pen are fluent and sure. Walter was clearly a natural, but he didn't stay and let his family see his talent bud – he vanished in a Texas sunset, a free spirit as they called him disparagingly when his name was uttered, which was infrequently.

Did Deaf Walter feel the shame that I felt heaping up in me, that this innate gift hadn't any value in the culture unless it generated mega cash, the creeping sense that a writerartist's mere existence is a queer mistake because its place and the marketplace aren't always the same place? In fact, where the market isn't – is there such a place?

The shame is thick, sticky and invisible in a writerartist. It's a feat, getting it unstuck – well, first seeing it at all, as a separate entity itself that isn't actually a built-in birthright. Shame is like ivy that creeps up a tree. It's hard telling which is the ivy and which is the tree. Tree experts tell us that the ivy strangles terribly. Hacking away, the daily shame-hacking, the many days it wins and paralyses and fills a writerartist with self-hatred, hesitancy, and the packing-it-in threat menacing.

A friend sends hyperlinks, *The Elusive Creative Genius* and *Success, Failure and Writing*, TED talks by the writer Elizabeth

Gilbert. She has useful insights as much as is manageable in the mirthy, breathless, entertaining style that is de rigueur in the TED talk, in hand with the all-black garments and the stage-prancing.

When dealing with fear, failure and bad mental health as artist's dilemmas, Gilbert muses why her father, a chemical engineer, wasn't ever asked if he was afraid when chemical engineering as she, Elizabeth Gilbert, is asked if she is afraid when writing, especially after making vast sums with a particular NY *Times* paperback bestseller. The parallel she sets up, writerartist-chemical engineer is a bit funny, but any deeper insight remains elusive.

What she misses, perhaps evades, is shame. Chemical engineering isn't a pursuit that elicits shame in capitalism. It's a respectable career path. While many chemical engineers may experience shame, it isn't likely because they ticked 'chemical engineering' when selecting their academic subject. The numberless writerartist deaths by suicide, substance abuse, the mental illnesses are surely, in part, linked with this unrelenting shame. The art pursuit as a value-making life way has little value within capitalism *per se* unless big-cash-making. This grinds creativity with its pressures.

In Gilbert's TED talks she frequently brings up her 'freakish success', meaning the large funds she accrued by selling many paperbacks. Her next paperback was a 'failure' as it didn't sell much. The next was 'well-received', which means big sales.

It's quite amazing this, her sharp, inquiring mind and its refusal in challenging the publishing premises it exists within. Dubravka Ugrešić:

> Many serious writers are convinced that their ability to penetrate the market is a measure of their quality.[25]

Perhaps it isn't a surprise, given the massive benefits this system has given this writer. But it'd be really ballsy if a writerartist with capital status like Gilbert's, challenged the cash-related success/failure paradigm and delineated success's truer definings.

Aligning with writerartists that are thriving in their entirety, that have lives making and writing despite everything, watching their lives and ways and figurings is a shame cure. Reading them, their diaries, tracts, hearing their lectures, watching their interviews, films, life tales, figuring their living strategies. This helps keep a writerartist suicide-free while standing with writerartists in their fragilities, waywardnesses – their many and justified despairs – as we are all in the swirling shame swamp, which the Twitter feed isn't reflecting.

When I was WHAT I CALL MY American SELF, I was frequently asked first: what did I paint and next, what were my paintings' prices and where did I sell them? This was a challenge. In the first instance, I'd say that I painted real things but I painted abstract things as well. That was an issue as what's needed is a quick pitch with nil twists and nil clashes. In the latter instance, I'd get stuck and fumble as I didn't sell my paintings with any regularity, and their prices varied. I mightn't remember what prices they were. But deeper than that was the difficulty in feeling that my paintings' value was linked with their sales. That my existence as an artist was affirmed by selling. This didn't feel right. I was immediately smalled in that view (I smalled myself), yet it was a pervasive attitude.

It was true that paintings I valued greatly by certain artists did sell well at times, with prices that were high. Equally there were bestselling writers I eagerly read. But it is true that there were paintings by certain artists I deeply admired that didn't sell at all and there were writers that lacked sales, prizes and fame, yet they were brilliant, fresh and essential. They were insignificant in market terms and highly valuable in artistic measures. The market and the writerartist were divergent. Where did I situate myself?

Sell. Ancient English: *sellan* (verb), 'give up'.

When it seemed that all the artists I knew were gallery-hungry and sales-needy and all the writers I knew were seeking agents, fame, prizes, grants and bestseller status, it became like a ruthless survival game in a desert with back-stabbers hiding behind trees and in grassy ditches. When all the gatherings I attended seemed filled with writerartists that talked seemingly with me, but their eyes drifted behind me, circling the place, seeking agents that might help their careers, and when I saw in myself the same tendencies even when I hadn't anything that was truly well made, and I feared anything durable in me might be terminally mislaid by this ghastly bent, I ran away.

I wanted myself free inasmuch as I first needed myself as vessel. A vessel that might have me-capacity. This isn't as easy as it might seem, when the vessel material has been a bit – perhaps even substantially – damaged. Perhaps certain vessel material is inherently flimsier and might require certain frequencies and temperatures unneeded by different vessel materials. The way I saw it, the culture I landed in assumed all its members thrived in similar circumstances, and I felt myself dying in it. In the selling-market culture I was sinking fast, my me flying away in the wild blue like a scared bird. I grabbed its tail and held, Ireland-enabled.

I wanted the vessel but was impatient and resisted the time it takes, the much time and many failures and mistakes in figuring what will be in the actual vessel. In my case it meant walking (it seemed) every path that wasn't my path as a deciding technique. Finding what I might keep putting in the vessel and what fits the vessel; that is the success part. This has taken much time. In different lives, it takes less time. Every life is different. When the vessel has been tested and isn't very leaky, then it's primed.

Pitfall: the cash-making paths taken; the attempted pursuits in career paths that are slightly acceptable that are in the arts/language fields. Teaching, lecturing, museum, library and arts centre placements, editing, publishing, arts-administering, design, managing literary and arts festivals. In ways, it is 'keeping a hand in', an adjacent pursuit as a rent-paying means. Adjacent pursuits which are actually distant pursuits if art isn't being made in the meantimes if that is what the vessel demands. Requires much trial and failure.

Time is the linchpin. Priceless time. The making craft requires time that capital eats up daily. Demands daydreaming, failure and dead ends, chasing fanciful things that can't yield anything except in far far distant time. Creativity's time isn't marketplace time and isn't manufacturing time and these things are waged against us. Art isn't efficient. Yet is fruitful, fecund, fertile. Is a Venus Genetrix.

85

The thesaurus teaches me a new term: a *fletcher* makes and sells sharp implements used in hunting in the days when there weren't any guns, which in my New Jersey area wasn't very far in the past. The Lenni Lenape were highly skilled fletchers, because my sylvan New Jersey play areas were littered with the small and sharp lithic heads they used in felling prey – deer, birds, squirrels, bear, fish – and human enemies. Urban Farms was where the Lenni Lenape camped and hunted where the wildlife was plentiful in the dense trees and the freshwater lake. Their paths linked up there.

When my father and Pat Canavan were building the bar in Patersin in the years after the war, they turned up the Lenni Lenape relics in their diggings. Pat, being a fine carpenter and an antique-gatherer, saved seven and put them in a packet sealed with paper tape. The bar they built later became a restaurant then a catering hall and a very successful business. It was purchased by a family with mafia ties in the eighties and is where a reality TV thing takes place. Years later, after I inquired if the archaic fragments were still in existence, Pat's daughter sent me that packet saying she'd rather they be appreciated than having them sit in a drawer. There are the seven sharp things beside me here. They're like little lithic Christmas trees.

Each chert, flint and quartzite piece is finely cut – the term is 'flintknapped' – by hand, and has a distinct shape. These scrapers, darts, knife blades and spearheads may have been in existence 14,000 years. Maybe 300. Each surface details the multiple hits an earlier man exerted. There is a tall thin piece that is exactly my pinkie's length and nearly as wide, and is a deep rusty umber hue; it might have been a spearhead, which was inserted in an atlatl – a spear-launcher – and chucked with great speed. The tiniest is half that length and is a warm grey flint; it must have had a small bird as its intended quarry. These little death implements sustained the Lenni Lenape's lives. Death by hunger, by disease, by extreme weather was a daily threat; death was braided in their lives, a perpetual whisper at their ears in every living, breathing instant.

Their hands and their skill. Their hunger and their need – what impelled their hunting. Hunger and need impelled my granny, in leaving Curraghard and her family, taking a ship with her sister, facing a vastly different future as a wealthy NYC family's servant girl and later, as a tinsmith's wife. She was a scrubber. My aunt remembers my granny's bare knees scraped raw as she scrubbed the hearth while my grandfather sat in his recliner in silk pyjamas with his pipe, reading the newspaper.

I sit at my Ikea writing desk in Ireland with these ancient American traces in my hand. Their surfaces are gently faceted by carefully crafted chisel hits. I'm aware that each little mark was handmade by an individual and that these individuals lived where I lived but deeper in the past, a layer beneath the layer where I exist. Such vastly different universes, a blaring fact which is evident and hidden at the same time. I try squaring Urban Farms and the Lenni Lenape, and my head bursts. We didn't inhabit that land; we garnished it. Fanny H. says the difficulty is being American. I think she means that future-leaning quality, that yesteryear blindness, that inward gaze which refuses the larger planetary view, refuses the past. It is a haunted place, that place I evacuated. These fletcher relics incarnate the gaping space between life and the lifestyle we lived in that strange place where death was erased.

The edges are still sharp, might still kill if catapulted.

86

My parents are sweethearts in a car park in Patersin in the black-and-white picture. She is jumping, tucking knees up under her smart A-line dress hem, making them disappear. My father, with admirable ease, balances her in mid-air by gently lifting her up at her bending arms as in an unrehearsed *pas de deux*. He's wearing a trilby, a well-cut suit with widely cuffed pants, and his feet are planted firm in a wide stance. He has a 1940s swagger like he can't believe his luck with this dame. Her fingers are held upright in a delicate gesture making 2 white lilies. She is wearing a jaunty felt tam that's spilling wiry reddish curls. They are all haberdashery and finery in their Sunday best. Their smiles are teethy and unabashed. In the next years they will marry and he will enlist in the US Navy where he will be flagman in the war while she lives in the triple-decker with his parents and his sister and her husband. And waits.

Behind them is a car that's being repaired, with trilby-ed Pat Canavan, his high receding hairline, peering beneath the upraised metal grille and behind that the street. A fruit truck is making a delivery. Gas lamps, their urban American shapes, pepper the upper street scene. The sun is sharp, angled, it's late in the day – autumn, given their garments. Perhaps it's Easter.

The picture's meaning in my life had changed. Rather than being a thing that represented my dead parents, a reminder, it became a talking piece with my guests, a fascinating item. It was causing chuckles, which disturbed me. Abruptly, I switched where it was displayed. It left the hall where it had been in public view, and I put it instead in my study, beside me here at the white table where I write.

Beneath the linen lampshade during the early evenings in my study, my parents' picture began making a little din. It was emitting these surprising little clicks. Maybe a change in the humidity and the light bulb's heat was causing it? My carefree parents. They had been silent and glassed-in and were suddenly animate. Tap-tapping. Saying 'hey!' It might have meant anything but what I decide it means, this parental tumult, is that there was a time when they were happy. They had waded all the way in the heart-depth, that pair. They had felt heartbreak and they had felt heart-depth. They wanted my seeing them in their living bliss.

I see.

87

The painting act is very strange when viewed in detail.

What I want is a refulgent underpainting. There must be a live wire, pulsing-hued presence beneath this self-study's tempered surface because that is the way this figure feels: undead, vivid, humming with fierceness under the surface. Yet that isn't her entire tint. The painting must feel like the vital fluids circulating after a swim in seven degree Celsius saltwater buried beneath a pale, undulatingly pinkish-bluish skin layer.

> Notes de n'importe quoi: the whites of her eyes were blue like
> the skin of a little silverfish lit from inside.
> —Eileen Gray[26]

Apply a wash in alizarin and turp. Let it sit and dry a day. A brash, pink statement with Titanium White lighting it beneath. The substratum's material must be well-appraised and must be perceivable and felt in the finished picture even if subtle as hell.

Return the next day because this isn't an Instagram enthusiasm; we're making actual things here. The place is fragranced already by painting, which means we are in the material realms. Richard D.'s dictum was that the day's first view is always when sight is clearest, freshest, but in this early stage, there's little that strikes except the single-hued alizarin punch in the plexus.

Table at the right: a glass palette and twisted metal paint tubes in a pile.

Squeeze:

Lamp Black
Jaune Brillant
Mustard Earth
Venetian Red
Burnt Sienna
Raw Sienna
Burnt Umber
Raw Umber
Ultramarine Blue
Payne's Grey
Unbleached Titanium
Flake White
Zinc White

A limited, mainly earth-hued palette, all in little piles at the glass palette's edges. A limited palette because this is a bleached linen language requiring scrutiny, silken silence and daring.

Mix sun-thickened linseed (stand) with turpentine in a baby Pablum jar, which makes a medium, a carrier. Actually it is like saliva in the way that a finger is wetted when turning a page. It advances things. I like mixing in wax, just a little clump, as it lessens the surface's sheen when the painting is dry, aligns the painting with bees.

Take a palette knife and mix Raw Umber with a little Zinc. Pick up a filbert brush, maybe size eight, dip it in medium then the mix. View the eyes. Place them generally, their setting and attitude. Be careful and precise with their angle because the eyes are never level and same-sized. My left eye is less awake, heavier-lidded; the right eye is wider, brighter, arched with an ample lid, mimics the way I am inside.

The left eye is the sinister, inward, guarded part that keeps shtum. It values secludedness, is frequently withdrawn and takes pleasure in apartness. The left eye is hidden behind hedges. Quiet, minimal, it likes laundry gently thwapping in breezes, dim lighting, stews and baking, dusting, cleaning with vinegar, everything in its place – these the left eye thrives in. The left eye dislikes buzzers – they signal intruders. If I had just my left eye and lacked my right, I'd be in a self-made, beautiful cave, hiding and biting at any that came near threatening my apartness.

The right eye is unbarred, leaking. Anything in the right eye's path is affiliated with it. The right eye relishes what impresses its retina; it unites with all realms that it sees and it isn't discerning. In this eye, my hue-mixing talent lies; in this eye I unite with everything that isn't me, which has been tricky. In this eye, I perceive pure beauty and danger, I scrutinize and inquire. The right eye hasn't any fences. The right eye is a right slut. If I had just my right eye and lacked my left I'd be a human being-shaped vacant space, having leaked away and united with the planet's furnishings and inhabitants.

It's lucky I have this eye pair even if they are askew and asymmetrical. A necessary mismatch. The right and left eyes are clashing partners serving as my superglue; they are the resin and the hardener that, when mixed, adhere this fragmentary being.

88

The painter Philip G. began life in 1913 in Canada. He was number seven, the last child in his big family. His parents, Rachel and Leib, had fled the Jew-murders in current-day Ukraine years earlier. Canada, being freezing, was a challenge – the Gs were a temperate Black Sea family. In 1919, seeking a better climate than Canada's, the family upped sticks and arrived in sunny LA, CA.

Leib had been trained as a blacksmith in Russia but had a hard time getting hired in that trade in his new life. In LA, he became a junkman. He travelled LA's backstreets and picked up garbage and unwanted stuff with a cart and a nag at the helm. Perhaps, when picking up refuse and unwanted stuff, it is difficult separating a self and the awful shit the self must undertake when there is a big family needing fed. Perhaps a sunny climate magnified the garbage stench and his dilemma. Whatever the cause, Leib grew increasingly dispirited and, sadly, he reached his limit: he hung himself. It was Philip, tender-aged eleven, that entered the shed and saw his dead dad there, suspended. Philip's being was deeply scarred by this image. He was seared by the trauma and the bereavement.

As a thirteenth birthday present, Rachel matriculated Philip in drawing-classes-by-mail that were run by an institute in Cleveland. A year later, he entered Manual Arts High where he met J.P., the Big Splasher-Dripper. He did a few years at the Art Institute in LA but didn't finish. Then Wall Street crashed. Philip became interested in activism and justice issues. In LA in the 1920s, the Ku Klux Klan were very visible and had sheriffs and bigwigs in their membership; they marched in the streets in their weird get-ups, acted as strike-breakers. They attacked Basque immigrants that were making whisky in a still and killed a sheriff while they were at it. Thirty-seven Klansmen were arrested in that raid – many were civil servants. All were acquitted. These threatening hateful gangs recalled the Jew-murderers in Russia and Ukraine that his family had fled and that surely had haunted Philip's father.

Philip was inspired by the great justice-hungry Mexican muralists. He travelled there, viewed the murals and painted them there as well. As he educated himself in painting, Philip was taken by the fifteenth-century Italian muralists, as well as the Mexicans. Philip was feeding his right eye.

In the 1940s, in NYC, Philip made many murals in FDR's New Deal artist scheme, the WPA. This was a big change time. He left his Jewish name behind and re-surnamed himself. He married the writerartist Musa McKim, his life's muse. Then the restlessness set in. He grew tired making mural paintings in big architectural spaces with artist teams and their intrigues, spats and intricacies. He wanted independent time, making individual paintings. Philip's left eye was hungry.

Philip and Musa left Manhattan and headed upstate. WWII raged. Philip began making abstract paintings, very light-hued, ethereal, airy yet meaty things. Large. In 1949 Philip was awarded the Prix de Italy and travelled there with Musa and their daughter Musa where he saw the amazing paintings first hand. They seared his retinas.

Back in NYC after that Italian year, Philip rented a making-place in the Village and dug himself deeply inside the painting activity. He was active but wasn't selling much. Between 1948 and 1956, he made 2 painting sales. Then the NY Abstracters came up as the 1950s advanced. They were a painting bunch linked with jazz, NYC, abstractness, the New. They were men, pretty much. Philip was put in this class, perhaps reluctantly, but his fame increased. Success aka cash began arriving via painting sales; the sales were rising. There was a big swell making a big wave and P.G. was right in there with the big surfers. Critics were writing, party invites were plentiful, he was in demand as a teacher and exhibiter. Philip was a made painter.

But in Philip's creative apparatus an inner disagreement started emerging: he began viewing his earlier, 'realer' paintings with renewed interest. The 'pure' abstract paintings weren't sustaining him, they seemed mannered and lacked urgency. What was happening, he mused, and asked Musa.

She said, *A rhythm is a tune and a rhythm is a rut.*

Which is it, Philip?

I remember days of doing pure drawings immediately followed by days of doing the other – drawings of objects. It wasn't a transition in the way it was in 1948 when one feeling was fading away and a new one had not yet been born. It was two equally powerful impulses at loggerheads.[27]

It was pretty bewildering. A crisis gripped him; he gave up painting and just drew in his little upstate shed. He spent a few years drawing real things.

What I think happened is that Philip began seeing with his right and left eyes. He decided that he must have the pair. He tacked up the nag and the cart and was keeping the reins, the left and the right eyes, in his hands. His junkman dad's cart was revving up and bringing him new things that he'd never have seen with either, single eye. He needed the clash, the gainsaying sight that led him in this new path. The paintings he made after that became his signature. They are the strangest, awkwardest, clunkiest things made with sensual, fleshy brushings. Cigarette butts piled up. Lightbulbs hanging. Musa's hair parted in the middle, writ large. A little barbecue grill raging in a dark landscape. Cherries piled up near a ledge under a blue sky. Ku Klux Klan gangs in G-man sunglasses with cigarettes in their fat mitts driving in brazen cars, wing-tipped, victim legs jutting at the back.

It seems the artist's task is seeing clearly with the left and the right eyes. Evil – in its varying trickster guises, in sweepingly large, cultural events (e.g., ethnic cleansings) and small, everyday stupidities (e.g., child neglect) – exerts such pressure that an eye can't help but shut. A split results. That refused, unseen thing waits in darkness. Creative energy can result in that clash when that eye, having been shut by pain, can let light in again and see.

Let us end this chapter in the city where Philip G.'s parents lived and suffered and fled, where lived Isaac Babel, aged ten in 1905. When anti-Semitism was running high in that Black Sea city, Isaac braved the public market and purchased his little heart's desire: a pet bird. In the street, he met a citizen riled up with Jew-hatred that landed Isaac with an awful punch. The lad and the bird he held, crumpled:

> I lay on the ground, and the guts of the crushed bird trickled down from my temple. They flowed down my cheek, winding this way and that, splashing, blinding me. The tender pigeon-guts slid down over my forehead, and I closed my solitary unstopped-up eye so as not to see the world that spread out before me. This world was tiny, and it was awful.[28]

Twenty years later, writer Isaac Babel unbarred that eye and penned the remarkable tale, which Philip G. read as he painted his remarkable late pictures.

89

Measure the space between the eye and the hairline.

Find the hairline's map edge, trace it, every quiver, every inlet.

Then trace the meandering line where lips meet. Mark the dark dimples beneath the lips.

A start, a placing. A stab at fixing this fleeting, smithereened, vacillating thing that is a self viewing a self. Take a step back and mull.

It rarely feels right at the start. Likelier, it feels perched at failure's edge-ledge, inexpert, inexperienced. As time and painting experiences increase, the familiarity with uneasiness increases but the uneasiness itself rarely decreases.

These attempts advance things. Relativities establish. Painting is heeding interrelatedness, seeing all the parts that make up the scene, marking them, making them physical.

Behind, in the way way back, the linen lampshade rhymes a little with this face hue but it's much greyer. Take Raw Umber, mix in Zinc and add the already mixed hue.

Put it up there and see. Stand back.

I resemble a bird, a garden-variety bird, in the way my head flicks – the painting, the scene, the palette, the painting, the palette, the scene, then a dance-step back, a glance up. Sharp, nervy neck flicks.

The painting is talking back, answering all the little raids I'm making.

It instructs in keeping things unfixed the entire painting time.

The thing shuts up if things are set early. Ceases giving back.

The painting says that the back wall is bluish like the iris in my eye.

I and the wall are related.

Testing and seeing is the way. I can't think this. It is a seeing game. The jumper grey is the right value, darker than my face mainly, but same value as under-chin area. Yep, that's better. Maybe it isn't the final but it's inching there.

The painting is under way. An interchange.

The brush and where it is held: near the tip and I'm near the painting's surface when what is needed is careful and precise. In that nearness I breathe in the surface and its linseedy smell. This isn't frequent. Generally the brush is held at its near end in such a way that I am less in charge. The brush is akin with a divining stick – it quivers and falls, when twisted, it can jump and skibble, be unpredictable, which is a friendly brush quality, an animated and kindly presence. A wide brush is like a digger: it can clear the field in a minute, levelling all the earlier brushings. Then a palette knife scrapes the remaining paint, and the field is ready. Re-think. Re-see. Re-feel. Enter the painting-jungle deeper, every preliminary brush mark a signal that leads in the painting's drift. It's a maze. It's a map that leads me astray infinitely. It's an infinitely fluid medium.

> Weakness is great, strength is insignificant. When man is born he is weak and malleable. When he dies he is strong and callused. When a tree is still growing it is flexible and tender, and when it is dry and hard, it dies. Callosity and strength are the companions of death. Pliancy and weakness are signs of the freshness of being. What has grown hard will therefore never triumph.
> —Lao Tsu, handwritten in Andrei T.'s diary,
> 28 December 1977.[29]

90

Perhaps it is their inbuilt distancing, a craft requirement, their dedicated stance being behind a viewing lens that renders them perpetually apart. They enter the heart's chalk circle, make credible marks but then depart, can't stay within, run back behind their lenses, tri-legged camera stands, their easels, tables, screens and plinths. The Rick Three-Sticks that have marked my heart.

Perhaps. But maybe truer is that a distancing apparatus has set itself up inside me. An inbuilt arms'-length machine that I need (safety) and that I eschew (wanting enlargement). It has certainly magnetized me with the Rick Three-Sticks. We share a detachment art. Yes, I am a Rick Three-Sticks as well. The hearts I have marked.

Perhaps it is Mike Zwick redux, a life refrain that spawned in me when I kneeled and peered and pined as a girl with awakening desires, grasping at that (wanted) thing in quick glimpses. Perhaps, it tuned me in a restrained key that has affected me intimately.

There had been charm, much charm. Quips, jests, quick intelligent teases that made me laugh. He was a news junkie, a lefty, had a quick mind a quick wit. After having met a few times with friends we met and leaned at a busy bar. I sipped white wine in a stemless glass while Rick drank Guinness in a chubby pint measure. Because it was rackety, he leaned in and talked in my hair. When I replied in his ample ear, I examined his cheekskin, black little stubbles in it like a hastily clear-cut timber tract, inspected his skewed teeth that were like Scrabble tiles placed carelessly in their stand. His dark, water-seer's eyes were implausibly large like a seal's, like lenses at full aperture. When they darted left, I saw slight ridges that limned the plastic lenses lying in them. Rick was vainer than he first seemed. I learned this later. As he talked, I was awash in his breath. It hadn't any smell, a sign that there was physical agreement between us. Certain breath hasn't a smell in the way that native district accents are undetectable and familiar.

It was Rick Three-Sticks' kisses that made me stay. He had this lingual fluency, a delicacy that disarmed, made my defences crumple. In the street, in the thinning darkness when we first kissed, it was as if he was talking silently in my lips saying the sweetest things in many languages. I'd lean back, part my jaws and plummet. What a relief, that descent. It was such pleasure that made me adhere. We were unrestrained and animal, made perfect intimate vignettes that I still carry in a cache. Perhaps every human carries such scenes in a cache.

Rick Three-Sticks was adept at very pulled-in camera angles that starred us. In these scenes, he was unbarred with that silent talking and actual language that was rightly tuned. But few are the films that lack any wide perspectives. After the ravishing tight studies, Rick scrammed. Ran. Rick stashed himself safely back behind his trusty lens. I'd be left – reamed at heart level and puddled in bedlinens. I'd crave and crave, which kept him farther and farther away, remaining in his lens shed. And this refrain refrained in endless, repetitive varieties. A familiar human pattern: I've read the studies.

It was fascinating as well. When I'd be left in Rick's bed beneath the ungainly duvet, when he departed and I was abed, bereft, I peered beneath and spied clear plastic crates that held letters in their hundreds. He saved them, his ex-girlfriends' missives, their pleas, their strandednesses, their detailing all the ways they wanted him, their kiss-deprivings, their sweet rememberings, little trinkets, creased pentimenti, tram, gig and screening tickets all tucked inside. There were pictures as well, snapped in Airbnbs in Dakar, Madagascar, Damascus, Austin, Cannes, Zagreb. The many divine and beddable girlfriends beneath Rick Three-Sticks' bed!

I believe that while Rick sleeps the spent girlfriends' letters beneath the bed emit a united, high-pitched wail imperceptible except at Rick's particularly detached wavelength. The ex-girlfriend din is a click-track that pierces his inner ear like an ice pick, excites him in his mundane days and recharges him at night when the track has weakened, enabling the split state he lives in.

Beneath that bed is an intimate museum. It is all in the dusty, distant past. There am I as well, preserved and filed in that weird Dewey Decimal dark. The Rick Three-Sticks intimate-distance dilemma.

91

All the significant activity is executed at the brush tip and just a little distance up the bristles. The painter must be extremely prudent with paint quantity. A beginner will dip the brush deep in paint, thinking, That's what's needed, right? Paint! Then the paint is drawn up and gets jammed high in the bristles. Cleaning there is hard. Paint will dry in that dense bristle-glade beneath the metal ferrule and stiffen the brush. The ferrule will be marred, which is a shame as a shining ferrule is a beautiful thing. The upper brush area is exclusively a structure that enables a paint brush's agency; it isn't actively engaged in making marks. Painters learn this by experience.

Painting is a pressure game. Fineness is achieved utilizing the bristles as if they were feathers, as if the brush were whispering the tenderest things. It feels a privilege when brushing this way. That any artist, that any brush-wielding being, has this chance at being attentive, is a delight. It is as if breath is being transubstantiated in line. When painting a fine line, the painter inhales and retains her breath; then exhales it thinly in the bristles in her brush-wielding hand. The line that results has humanized air in it. This can happen with fine pencil line drawing as well. Rembrandt excelled at this; inspect the feathers in Saskia's fancy hat. Van Rijn's exhalings are there in the drawn wisps.

Running fingers in her lavish hair was a satisfying practice, being tactile, being present. In fact being tactile and present in her lengths and widths entirely was a privilege. She was herself well-versed in caresses, in tight spaces, in whisper distances. Her sternum was wide and flat like a halberd that made her seem at times fierce and unfuckable, and at times it was a wide table at which my presence was requested. Beneath that sternum was a well-muscled heart that had been examined, exercised, stretched and tested. It knew itself as much as a heart might, which isn't ever fully settled. There are always unmapped tracts. I surprised myself getting in very tight, examining each freckle, wrinkle, piercing-scar. Being with Saskia was fine; I felt myself unfettered.

We were quite alike. Each had sturdy, plentiful hair, dark and light in hue: badger-ish. We had light caresses, light laughs. We blended easily, matching each with each and matching whatever milieu we entered. Saskia simulated me and I simulated Saskia. We were genuine. We imitated. Were intimate. United. A unit. Saskia and I behaved as paintbrushes parallel in a tray.

Painting requires that an artist shed all defences, unite with her subject. Be engulfed. Intimacy, I fear, requires the same. I left Saskia, fearing being annihilated in her and by her. The Saskia intimate-engulfment dilemma.

92

Mary Blessed Sacrament, Urban Farms after Sunday mass in the springtime, Easter-ish. Families are hurrying, packing themselves in their large cars. In their minds are massive newspapers, scrambled eggs, crumb buns, breakfast tea and all the Sunday treats in their immediate futures. Perhaps drink a Virgin Mary with a celery stirrer. But first there is a terrier puppy that has been shut up in a car during Mass, and it's been let run in the grass verges. I remember bending in dewy grass, hugging that mutt tight beneath its plump, milk-warm, wiry-haired belly and making a face I've made many times since. I call it (inside myself) the Mutt-Mass-Car-Park Face. It's easy: I just bite my lip hard with my upper teeth and scrunch up my face a little. It isn't just a facial gesture; it's an entire system-undertaking. I squeeze my centre muscles and rev up deep pleasure – that I must sniff and inspect this life like that mutt.

93

The island flares in the sunlit sea like a silver penny adrift. Streedagh, where the waves are turbulent, where the Spanish Armada sank, where its wrecked fleet is still interred in the beach, is the nearest mainland bit, but that is still seven km distant.

Inishmurray is far, flat, discreet, stranded; an ascetic's island. At my life's end my ashes will be scattered there. I will then infiltrate it entirely.

I'd get there by swimming if I were able, but its distance impedes my desire. Instead, I bring my friend and her friend and their girls. We take a fishing cruiser captained by Ultan. I wield as large a drawing tablet as I can manage. It frequently catches the ample wind, nearly taking me with it. Pretending I am a sail and delighting in partially depicting a sailing vessel, I name all the rigs I can: square-rigger, brig, barque, barquentine, caravel, clipper, nef. The nautical terms have a tasty, chewy feel when said: luff, baggywrinkle, cleat, clew lines, furl, jib, leech, spinnaker, mainsail, mainsheet.

My drawing tablet-cum-sail is handmade – Rives BFK printmaking paper sheets, the best paper there is. I fastened them myself with mercerized twine.

Pencils and charred vine in a sack in my parka. Gummy rubber. All that's needed.

~~The Annals tell us Inishmurray was settled by ascetics in the sixth century; they lived there until the twelfth century. Within the Cashel is their church, the Teampeall na Tine, a beehive hut, a~~

~~kitchen building, sleeping chambers and many altars, leachta, with their cursing/blessing devices. The Cashel's walls are high and thick, which tell that the Vikings attacked and pillaged the island.~~

~~The raids began in the ninth century and it may be what made them leave eventually.[30]~~

Halt.

That may be true yet I repudiate the Baedecker style.

Draw nearer the landing place, Clashybeg, a name that is a little bit menacing. Ultan glides the craft in then abruptly reverses the engine. With the running tide the yawl is steady, and I

jump

clear the gap, help the rest debark and wave at Ultan (he's away fishing until sunset).

Feel the island beneath my feet, its sheer reliability amid the agitated sea.

First seen thing after the landing's flat flags: hairballs spat up by the hunting birds that arrive at Inishmurray in the night. Whispery thin pencil lines in a skein like attenuated sheep's fleece caught in whin and whipped by the wind secured in that net. Fish and rabbit skeletal remains. Tiny curved, sharp crab claw pincer, lacy fish ribs, rabbit ulna, felted fur. What that bird's gullet didn't digest it threw up.

There are hairballs everywhere! The birds leave their nests at Lissadell in the night and hunt the island rabbits and fly back at dawn. Rabbits and birds are Inishmurray's inhabitants. Gulls, terns, kittiwakes. Puffins perhaps.

There are incredible intact altars with their carvings, beehive huts. The distance that Ben Bulben is is staggering.

The last families that inhabited Inishmurray left with their sheep and cattle in their sea crafts in 1948.

I saw the purplest jellyfish in the little inlet there. Ever.

Mackerel flash their sharp silver and black stripes, like underwater gangsters in knife fights, in Clashybeg.

We saw the girls climbing the nunnery's walls. They clambered up, held themselves high and erect, became church pinnacles. We didn't dare yell at them because they were statuesque and maybe predicted a new era in Ireland.

We wanted that.

Inishmurray Beliefs:

There is a little chapel there and it can never be filled up.

There are separate male and female burial places. If a dead man is buried in the female graveyard, the next day the remains will have been exhumed.

There are altars scattered in many places there. The altar near the chapel has many spherical lithics and their number never adds up as the same number twice. Try tallying them up. Then try again. The numbers will always be different.

Turning the lithics can create curses and blessings.

The sea between the island and the mainland is generally heavy. If an islander is sick, they take island well water and sprinkle it in the sea and it immediately calms until a wherry can bring a medic, and at times a priest, and the sick islander can be treated. When the wherry has island-returned after bringing the medic back, the sea gets turbulent again immediately.

Inishmurray is an ascetic island. I shun the chaste life. I thrive in it.

94

The death has taken place peacefully at her residence please chari-
table family members exclusively
  – suddenly
The death has taken place after an extended illness wireless emitting litanies deceased resting burial afterwards new cemetery
beside ancient
  – suddenly
The death has taken place residence private Sunday evening please
family deeply regretted by
  – suddenly
The death has taken place everything ceases every ear pricks we
can hear tick ticking tap eerily dripping
  – suddenly
The death has taken place cared by nurses and staff arrival at
quarter past predeceased by her granddaughter husband
  – suddenly
The death has taken place news airwaves arrives glum church
music track beneath dignified narrating sadly missed peacefully
  – suddenly

www.rip.ie lists the arrangements, whether the casket's ritual
church trip is private/public, what charities the family like, and,
crucially, a map detailing where the church and graveyard are.

Rural funerals are vest and vestment events. Vests are garments
that an individual can easily wear and are a signal that s/he has a

special part in the funeral ritual. Vestments are priest garb, such as chasubles, which signal they have special parts as well in funerals, especially in the requiem mass and burial. But vests and vestments aren't the same.

But first, rural funerals must be arrived at. Pre-GPS, attending a funeral meant much time spent labyrinthing in rural Bermuda Triangles, driving hedged-in miles, passing samey, farmy stretches, thinking the church is just past the next bend, amazed that churches even existed there, that there were sufficient citizens that filled churches in these sparse places, that there were sufficient priests that might man them. GPS has made finding rural funerals easier.

When men in high-vis vests are sighted, the funeral is within spitting distance. At times they are hired funerary service men, but usually they're friends chipping in. I have heard them talk:

He's got room for ten cars up there at the church, but peer inside them's that's coming and send them up the church if there's auld 'uns inside them that can't walk the distance.

Hey Ger, PRIEST CAR! [and then they wave it where the hurriedly made sign reads *VIP PARKING*].

When all the cars have been parked well, the high-vis gentlemen ball up their vests, cram them in their cars, then assemble near the church entrance and are simply funeral attendees again.

A female wearing a pressed yet flimsy vest stitched with a large crucifix at the back serves wafers at the funeral Mass. She is tasked with wading deep in the gathering at the church's rear and distributing the blessed crackers, which she carries in a shiny brass tray. When she's finished, she hangs the vest up in the priests' dressing chamber, and she is a public female again. She blends back in with the rest.

Priests lead the rituals at the funeral mass. Priests are always male in this sect, yet unlike the many males in rural funerals that are attired in black, grey and generally dun-hued garments, the priests wear purple and lavender vestments, shiny, gender-bending silks that are bias-cut with metallic detailing. Their white under-vestments are bleached and starched, usually by females that attend the priests and clean their apartments. Priests' vestments are eye-catching and signal their status as rite leaders. When priests aren't wearing their vestments, they are still priests, which is different than the traffic-directing and wafer-distributing vest-wearers at funerals.

There weren't dramatic, candle-flame twistings in the night wind in the village cemetery at Lughnasa. Candle wax wasn't hissing, leaping, extinguishing itself Slavically in the little graveyard at Killeenan. Glass lanterns huddled humbly inside the grave areas. Clear glass gave white light. Green glass gave chilly light. Red glass gave warm light. The lanterns burned with reserve. They didn't waver. Each flame was neatly capped with a Raw Umber-hued metal hat pierced by crucifix shapes. The flames burned inward as we carry the dead inward within us. The lanterns held tenderness as tenderness that has died is held in a being and is remembered and kept alive. In their numbers the candles seemed as if they were taming the gaping space between us and the dead. They glimmered like lit gems and at a distance gave in fact great beauty. Family members had cleaned their family graves exhaustively and lit lanterns. The graveyards were tidy but they weren't manicured. Perhaps a few families went a bit far, but it didn't matter. Days after the graveyards flickered with the candle embers after dark and the street lights seemed inane, shining as if they had vanquished the night. Well, the night fell anyway that autumn in Killeenan.

A culture isn't yet in full demise if its funerary rites are still alive. If a guy can give up a day's wages unregretfully, leave Durrus in Munster at five am and arrive at a chapel in Derriaghy in Ulster by eleven am, feel his presence is right and needed at his friend-he-hasn't-seen-in-five-years' father-in-law's funeral, then glimmers are warranted. When a place is aflame in dead-remembering candle-light in late autumn, betterment is winning. If a fiddle, guitar and a timber flute play 'The Mangled Badger' at an aged lady's graveside, there is a chance we aren't quite yet in end times.

95

This chapter deals with a painting but first there is a priest part. The diminutive painting is a few centimetres larger than my Mac Air's screen. It was made by a Sienese master painter in the fifteenth century in a cycle dealing with San Bernadine's life and his alleged miracles. Saint Bernadine aka Bernadine was a very dedicated priest that delivered schismatic speeches in Siena's main square and were attended by virtually the entire city.

Bernadine arrived as a baby in Siena in 1406 and by the time he was six, his parents were dead; he was a dreaded r-phan. He was taken in by nuns and, later, became a Franciscan priest – there were many in Siena in the fifteenth century. Bernadine had a big evangelical streak. It is said that his speech quality was creaky and gruff but still, he was celebrated as an amazing public speaker. His subjects were daily life issues, practical and ethical matters that were accessible and relatable by many; he didn't deal much with scripture. His talks were lengthy, lasting half a day at times. His speeches drew audiences that were bigger than what the Tuscan and Umbrian churches fitted. Bernadine had pulpits erected in public plazas; that way he was visible and higher up. He liked the limelight, being in his pulpit, preaching at dawn and getting believers riled up, inciting public burnings.

Bernadine was against same-sex sex. *Spit at them*, he advised his listeners when they met same-sex sexers. He didn't like Jews, either. *Usurers*, he said. He believed in witches and fuelled that ancient female hatred we are all familiar with. At his public lectures, audience members built vanity fires and threw in all the stuff that fed their senses: perfumes, sexy texts and trinkets, musical instruments, scented creams, high heels, lavish undergarments, games, playing cards, and paintings. *Sin! Sin! Sin! The Devil!* cried Bernadine spell-bindingly. *All this must be banished!*

Bernadine captured deep fear and dressed it in sanctified garments – a dynamic and heady energy. He kickstarted mass hatreds that are still stuck in the (partial) public mind in the twenty-first century. Bernadine was a fear-inducing mastermind. We can see a Bernadine-like legacy in the Irish Church still as we discuss exhuming mass 'illegitimate' baby graves in a Tuam septic tank in the year 2019.

Bernadine lived until he was fairly ancient. He travelled Italy and preached and preached. He invented the IHS sign – a must-have crucifix appendage these days. 'IHS' is JESUS in Greek – well, the first three letters. The Higher-Ups weren't happy with the IHS thing and accused heresy. There was a big trial but Bernadine was acquitted. A few years after he died, he was made a saint. Yes, a saint.

Let's have the painting part.

S. di P. (1406–81) was a successful painter in Siena. He fraternized with the Franciscan ascetics in the city, especially Bernadine. S. di P. made many paintings including a series that deals with miracles that Bernadine allegedly executed. Art critics haven't praised S. di P. much but I think they're mistaken. I think S. di P. is the best. Well, he and Fra A. It was S. di P.'s black-and-white sheep in the pen that thrilled me and rescued me in my anxiety-ridden state many years past when I visited the municipal museum in Siena. We share a wavelength, I guess, S. di P. and me.

What is this urge called that makes me melt and desire diving in the painting, uniting myself with what I see in these little panels, their images, hues, shapes, rhythms, textures, surfaces, diminutive scales? The feeling is bewildering especially when in the flesh with an S. di P. It is surely sexual – Bernadine mightn't like what I'm writing here, especially given that he's frequently depicted in my treasured S. di P. pictures, usually as a half-angel, a sharp-chinned, craggy-faced thing. His angel butt emits ethereal blue matter, a seraphic jet stream, that enables his skyward state. But S. di P. paintings in the flesh are few and far between. It is usually in digital screens that I study them and they create a less intense feeling. Maybe that's salutary.

His painting depicting Bernadine resuscitating a child that's fallen in a rain barrel is a small and landscape-shaped timber panel, painted with tempera and metallic leaf. I have never seen this painting in the flesh; it isn't in a public museum. It's pictured in a Sienese painting guide that I have had since I began painting again in my twenties. The Web has this image in a site that sells master painting duplicates – a pretty decent facsimile it seems but I can't truly say as I can't see it in the flesh. Anyway, the image has gripped me these many years because I guess it tells a deep true thing.

In my experience, deep true things are slanted in their interdependence with us. We and they are inextricably linked, but we can't view deep true things directly. They are there, stage left, in darkness. They creep up and insinuate themselves in times when we are receptive aka usually when we are in pain. They are suspended at the mind's edge, making little infrequent raids, then retreating, sinking in darkness until pain, fucking pain – a distraught heart, a heavy grief, a betrayal – digs them up again. Then we see the deep true things clearly; then the deep true things fleetingly disappear again. And it persists like this.

Time in the resuscitated-child painting is depicted the way time feels in the mind and, increasingly, the way physicists say time actually behaves. They say that everything exists at the same time, that sequence is purely artificial and is essentially determined by feelings. The past and present intermingle in us and in nature. S. di P. paints this miracle's events in layered, cyclical images that feel real. Time is depicted as a flickering thing, a substance that gathers fragments and binds them.

In the painting's centre is the rain barrel, which the artist presents as a squat, knee-high water receptacle – a large, chestnut-hued timber bucket, really. The barrel is upstage in the middle. It makes a single appearance. While its rainwater, shaped like a cerulean eye, flickers, the barrel itself is steady and secured in its central placement. It stands undisturbed and unblinking.

The child appears twice. His age, the annals tell us, is a year and a half. In the centre, in a red tunic, he has fallen in the barrel in his parents' absence. He is underwater and in immediate danger. His red tunic is greenish beneath the rainwater's surface. Terre Verte is definitely the pigment used in painting the nearly dead child's submerged face. He is pictured standing at the left as well – his tunic vivid incarnadine as the hue isn't blunted by the intervening rainwater – after his rescue by the saint, which isn't directly depicted. The child's hands are praying, his hair is flaxen and fluffy. He is half adult height and casting his eyes upward.

A reverent man (the father? a passer-by?) appears three times in the picture. He is descending a staircase at the panel's extreme right; then he is at the barrel's right side peering in at the submerged child; and he is at the left, reaching his hands in a caring attitude, beside the upright, un-wet kid. In each instance, his hands are praying.

The child's mam, in a white headscarf with black stripes – typical Sienese female headgear – and wearing a blue dress, appears twice. She is at the rain barrel's left side, nearly straddling it, bending and reaching. Her left hands breaks the water's surface beneath which her child lies. Then she is at the panel's left, kneeling, her arms in an embracing gesture, gazing at her rescued, resuscitated, standing-up child.

There is a lady with a yeller dress and yeller hair as well. I imagine she is the landlady, maybe a friend? She is in the panel's middle at the barrel's side, viewing the sunken child. And she is kneeling at the left where the revivified child stands, her hands praying, her chin lifted and gazing at the small figure in the sky.

Saint Bernadine is that small figure. He's depicted as a half-human/half-angelic figure in a flying superman attitude. Behind his head is a metallic leaf nimbus meaning he has special status. His face is greyish, wizened and his chin is very sharp. He is wearing his priest's tunic, well at least his upper half is. Beneath his belt, he emits fumes like a car with a muffler issue.

Bernadine, a hateful, hate-riling figure, is a false deity. Fall Bernadine. Please descend and have an earthly burning crash. Painter, sandpaper that false angel and paint sky where he was.

The painting is a deeply flawed thing.

And I crave it.

What is a fifteenth-century painting's use in the twenty-first century? Why am I bedevilled by this little panel depicting a cruel man's alleged miracle? Is it simply the beguiling hues, shape-rhythms and patterns that Clement Greenberg insists I be beguiled by?

Allmylife this painting has had me transfixed. Surely it is that child-underwater image, that arrested state. Surrendered and supine, the child is adrift, near-sunk but undead still. As was I, but dryly. With his bright hands – bright being nearer the surface – and his greenish submerged face, the child is alive yet in an in-between – dare I say *liminal* – time-space. His mam's hands reach – they even break the rainwater's surface – but they can't meet her child's hands. She isn't yanking her child's arm and rescuing him like I think she must. They remain in separate states. The landlady/friend's hands beseech and pray but remain passive and distant. The father/passer-by as well; praying and passive. They can't save him.

This rescue is the child's and the deity's task.

Trauma specialists distinguish this fugue state as the split where the self fragments and the feeling piece flees/freezes until such time as it can emerge safely when the danger has passed.

This numb state and its detached, measureless, staggering pain.

The painting gives the silent, freezing place I went a shape and an image. Viewing it directly, unflinchingly, gives me dry heaves.

The child in the rain barrel is safeguarded in a circular shape painted with an invaluable, sacred material. The shape is like a linseed, an eye. The shape is like an alphabet letter – my name has a pair. The shape is a barrel as well. The circle-shape has saved and preserved the child's living energy. Yet the circle keeps him apart.

The child's hands aren't tense and grasping; they are relaxed, palms up, acquiescent.

~~It is the child's task...~~

~~It is my and the deity's task~~

It is my task: turn palms up and lie back in the rainwater barrel where I am preserved, and where I am jailed.

Invite the unfalse deity in that my shelter might be punctured. Leak.

96

Early December. Sliabh an Iarainn dusted in verglas (bleachgreen). A rare freezing night has passed and the sun is returning. My garden is still green. Green in the hedges, green in the winter grass that is verdant, that isn't burned in the freeze. Higher, the ashes are speckled with red berries. Blackbirds scatter in desiccated beech leaves when I walk near. Blackbirds alight in ash branches waiting, stilling themselves as I pass. Berries redden their shit.

Sliabh an Iarainn in deep shade, such an unlikely shape, flat, rucked, startling with the sun rising behind. Sliabh an Iarainn a timepiece ticking away while we live these digitized lives, catch glimpses driving past. Cairns in the far hills, flaxen in the sun, taking its direct hit as they have millennially. They are timepieces as well. Squeezed between these megaliths, we shelter, bask, and grasp.

The grass is greening, talling even in winter. The vivid geranium in the glazed blue dish retains a few cerise petals, precise in their high-vis incandescence. The freezing is weaving in: glazing, greying, gripping. The freezing meets the wet in the air. Flicks ice and ashes it all. My garden flecked in freeze in this green place I live.

7

GALILEELEELEELEELEELEELEELEELEELEELY

97

Beginning is swimming. We are swimmers at the start and haematic breathers. We grew as a unit, my baby and me. As I grew bigger, she increased herself. She was held in place by my uterine muscles' fierce grip. She was fierce, generally. A runner and a shaker stirring inside me since she was sprat-sized, a being held under Sagittarius's sway.

She began as a marine creature breathing her vital fluids in my pelvis's warm cradle. My heartbeat was her life's rhythm and hers was heard in the spaces between my deeper, measured rhythms. She pressed her tiny arm against her universe's dark wall and was met by my tense muscles and behind them my flesh and skin. That I had a separate external surface was unimaginable. That she had an external aspect must have been surprising, as well. Later.

She is a result, begat by me and her father in authentic carnal pleasure and amalgamating desire. She is a YES, YES YES, which deeply aligns with her being. In her, her parents' mismatch assembles and makes a perfect fit. Whatever energies between him and me that repelled-attracted, making a shared life unviable, are usefully harnessed and gain strength and capability in her.

Her cells' multiple splittings built up until her brain, heart, guts and sex were, as they say, determined. Her life mustered with a mighty, assured energy. That she exists – with such lithe arms, gleaming, dark rivery hair, lit pale skin that betrays subterranean veins in her temples and a Leitrim-shaped birth mark at her nape – is given. She is vividly inevitable.

There was an unlimitedness in the way we began. A flesh-built infinity with deep beats that reverberate up the spine and the sternum. An internal, un-retinal, Venetian Red light uninflected by time, date, circumstance. A sanctum.

She assimilated my daily cadences, my calm stillness when asleep, my walking measures, the earthquakes when I jumped. Rumbles she later learned were a TV, a vacuum cleaner, a sewing machine, were sensed in vibrating pulses. She felt my clasped hands pressing my belly, which was her spatial limit. Until it changed.

Late in a waiting day in late autumn when Judge Judy was ruling the TV, everything began churning. Muscle walls that had held her began rippling and pummelling. I called her father and he raced his van up the N4 with us, the heat blasting. There were sudden ceasings in the ripplings, as well. In such stillnesses she might have sensed my increasing ... what shall I name it? Uncertainty? Hesitancy? Unsureness?

I think fear is the term.

Lying in that ward with an unfeeling midwife attending, my heels pressed in the metal stirrups while rain lashed the dark glass – night was a distant event seen as if in a screen at a faraway drive-in cinema – I gleaned that it wasn't a baby making its way and arriving smack in my quiet life but a human being. A daughter. My life, that had been until that instant a sealed circle with a tentative I in its castaway centre, was dying. I was being redefined. She might mean everything.

I hadn't anticipated this, I wasn't prepared. I was sieged by a deep freezing fear that expressed itself in every gland, every fluid, every cell in the being I knew as myself.

My baby girl stalled in my vagina. The pushing urge never arrived. The bully midwife had measured my cervix and demanded that pushing begin at ten centimetres even if the desire hadn't yet ignited in me. My baby was arriving full speed at me, and I hadn't yet felt that driving, birthing urge.

Her life's brute need was met with my unsurrendered state. In Delivery Suite A, in an infinitesimal instant, with the mint-green midwife figure beside me attending this arriving being's head, I reassessed. A clammy nauseating slackness permeated me as a pulsing and illuminated red sign caught my eye:

EXIT

Push, the mint-green blur said flatly as she sat beside me. (Between my pulsings she entered data at her nurse desk.)

I strained dutifully. My lungs gushed with an exhale, but my pelvic muscles were slack. I didn't feel like pushing. My baby remained stuck, her face's future Quigley-resemblance mashed in my vagina's ridged walls. I lay panting, then emitted primal screams I didn't think I had in me, at the awful predicament we were in.

My baby girl didn't get what *EXIT* meant. She didn't get language yet. She didn't, in fact, get what understanding was. But she sensed the savage capacity in that term, she felt it surge in her as it surged in me, in the maternal line. Chill and silent, it mingled in us. It became a thing, a fact, a trait that can run in a family. It curdled in the shiny, fat placenta that had been my baby's bed, which the curt midwife cut away and laid in a kidney dish.

After they had grabbed her by the temples with their stainless-steel instruments and yanked her free, when she gulped her first lungful, my baby gazed in my strange face and I gazed in hers. She was wild and screamed a wild scream. I held her, quaking and wailing, as she first sensed her external surfaces. Her skin – this new suit that ached, that wasn't as warm as I had been. Bright pink pincer marks raged at her temples in her pliant, thrawn head, a thing seeking its shape.

She lifted her hand's strange map shape and between pudgy fingers held my gaze. And held it and held it. Time crumpled. In that instant I felt my fear being eclipsed by my baby's fury and by her beauty, her life hunger. I traced the Leitrim-shaped birthmark at her nape and ran my finger in her ear's delicate seashell patterns. The flesh she is. She buried her apple head in my full breast, its warmth, and snuffled and sucked at my dark nipple. My new blue milk, fluent and plentiful, sprayed in her gullet, briefly settling in her windpipe. She spluttered, dribbled and gasped, punched my clavicle with a little fist. Then she drank the gushing milk and sucked harder.

98

I used it this evening in making crumbly walnut squares that were packed with dried cherries, and Lindt's finest 99 per cent dark stuff. The handle is Bakelite, Burnt Sienna-hued. It has a warm glimmer, like amber. Hex-shaped; there are six faces in the tubular handle. The edges are burnished by design and with use. It fits perfectly in my palm, warms it. Fastened in each end are 2 flat, spade-shaped steel ferrules. Engraved in the side is *PATENTED 11−12−29 MADE IN USA*. She was nine when it was designed. Thirteen years later, in 1942, she and my father married, and I imagine that is when she acquired this pastry blender, which is an eBay vintage item these days. Hipsters prize vintage things like this.

The tines, if that's what these expressive wires are called, are curved. They create seven arch shapes spaced unevenly a few centimetres apart. The designers determined seven as the right pastry-blending number. Eight might be excessive, might waste the heavy-gauge wire material; six might be stingy. Seven arched wire tines is the right number. This implement cuts the pastry better than ten fingers can because fingers have warmth that melts the butter, making the pastry heavy. The chilly steel tines cut the butter better and let it sit within the mix, keeping intact little butter pilules that melt in the baking, which makes flaky pastry. The wire tines are bent and skewed in a few places since the blender has been packed in bubble wrap and shipped many miles with me in the umpteen places I've lived. Imperfect implement I cherish.

I remember eating the apple pies, latticed cherry pies, peach pies, peach crumbles, chicken and turkey pies, biscuits, quiches, and pecan sandies she made with this implement. I remember saying *yuck* at the mincemeat pies she made with it, shunning them. I remember what she did with any extra pastry: cut it in strips, brushed them with melted butter, sprinkled spices and sugar, then twirled them in snail-shell shapes and baked them until dark caramelized sugar dripped and sizzled at their edges. The fragrance lingers in my senses still – I can feel its particular tickle in my nasal skin. Her baking is stamped in my feeling faculties. I ate the sweet snail-shell pastries greedily when they were warm, ruining my dinner appetite.

When I use her pastry blender, I imagine her wielding it as well, cutting butter and baker's vegetable fat. My arm bends and drives the implement in gestures I clearly remember her making, dancing with her.

In this dance we fill in the gaps her leaving early left; her silences.

The pastry blender is a utensil linking me and my daughter with her and my larger matriarchal baking line. My daughter and I bake – an activity we began early and have ever practised enthusiastically. Surely my granny baked with whatever grains and fats there were in Curraghard in the 1880s. Surely there was baking even if meagre. Wheatmeal cakes perhaps.

While I'm writing, the pastry blender sits in the shelf beside me, upended, a little awry wire still life, with a sustained narrative built in.

99

Later in the year, say late May early June, I'm blessedly acclima-
tized. Swimming isn't survival these days: it's retrieval. Skipping
the strand, ever sharp-shell watchful, I meet the sea at ankle height,
run at the breakers and dive. Wave after wave. Thundering thin
green-glass Atlantic sheets I shatter with my arms in a V. Instant
child. Thrill. Thrilling. Thrilled. Jumping. Twirling. Messing.
Laughing. Screeching. Spluttering. Gasping. Falling backwards in
an X, bum scraping sand, sandbagging my swimsuit, tide dragging me this way and that. I let it. Handstanding in sand and
getting upended by currents, gulping saltwater. Trailing seaweed
bracelets, necklets, anklets, belts. Stepping lightly, crab aware.
Little pinchers. Then treading water, paddling arms and legs – all
underwater but my masked eyes, which scan the strand (nearly
empty – a few walkers with canines), Ben Bulben rising behind
it, furred with green, mist-hatted. Water cradles, busts edges,
spreads me Atlantically, Japanly, Indianly, Arctically, Laccadively,
Mediterraneanly, Baltically, Tranquilitily, Chileanly, Bengally,
Blackly, Adriatically, Redly, Sargassily, Barentsly, Tyrrhenianly,
Deadly, Caspianly, Antarctically, Tasmanianly, Pacifically,
Fundily, Caribbeanly, Campechily, Biscayly, Celtically, Ligurianly,
Galileeleeleeleeleeleeleeleeleeleeleeleely.

Acknowledgments

My gratitude for time and resources to write: Arts Council of Ireland and Radcliffe Institute for Advanced Studies, Harvard University. For formative conversations/reflections in and around Byerly Hall: Peter Behrens, Judith Belzer, Shane Bobrycki, Elliott Colla, David Ferry, Luke Fowler, Wendy Gan, Ross Gay, Sarah Howe, Bill Hurst, George Tiger Liu, Valerie Massadian, Alyssa Mt. Pleasant, Michelle Ng, Michael Pollan, Lesley Sharp, Reiko Yamada. To Dr. Judith Vichniac's memory, a bouquet of violets.

Go raibh maith agaibh: The Yeats Society & director Susan O'Keeffe; Anna Leask; Martin Corr; Una Mannion, colleagues and students at the Yeats Academy, IT Sligo; Jo Holmwood and the Kids' Own crowd; the Irish Writers Centre Novel Fair.

Boundless appreciation: The Lilliput Press – Antony Farrell, Ruth Hallinan & Djinn von Noorden for book love & fastidious care; my editor Colm Farren for astuteness, clarity & banter in track changes; Fiachra McCarthy, Marianne Gunn-O'Connor, Peter O'Connell.

For friendship on land & sea: John Brady, Amber Hayes, Eileen Hughes, Justyn Hunia, Gail McConnell, Nick Miller, Afke Pieterse, Robin Whitmore, Martha van der Meulen and the swimmers; fellows Katherine, Susan, Erica and Judith; the neighbours; Ciaran Carson, exemplary artist, *riposi in pace*; Linda Norton, Fanny Howe, Maureen McLane, trans-Atlantic beacons; Nerissa Edwards, Mark & Gina Auriema, Rory O'Connor & Clare Muhm, *un gran abrazo*; Mo-Mo, keeper of archives. Immeasurable thanks and love: the Lyons clan, for big dinners & conga lines; Isa van Schaik, for embarkings; Hazel Walker, Claire McAree, Orla Mc Hardy, nae better; Fionna Murray, without whom, no book. Denise Lyons, unsurpassable sister & Michael Stoner, brother-in-more-than-law; and Caoimhe, my 'lake of shining waters'.

Notes

1 http://bergencountyhistory.org/Pages/franklinlakes.html.

2 O'Brien, Jean M., *Firsting and Lasting: Writing Indians Out of Existence in New England* (Minneapolis 2010).

3 Excerpt(s) from I HAD TROUBLE IN GETTING TO SOLLA SOLLEW by Dr. Seuss, Trademark TM and copyright © by Dr. Seuss Enterprises, L.P. 1965, renewed 1993. Used by permission of Random House Children's Books, a division of Penguin Random House LLC. All rights reserved.

4 'The Typewriter: An Informal History', http://www.ibm.com.

5 Meredith, William, [extracts throughout from the following poems:] 'Notes on One's Head'; 'Crossing Over'; 'Hazard Faces a Sunday in the Decline'; 'Dalhousie Farm' in *Effort at Speech: New and Selected Poems* (Evanston 1997).

6 Herbert, Zbigniew, *Barbarian in the Garden* (New York, 1985).

7 Graves, Robert, 'Flying Crooked', in *Collected Poems* (London 2000). Poem reprinted with permission of the estate of Robert Graves and Carcanet Press.

8 Tolstoy, Leo, *Anna Karenina* (source: Project Gutenberg).

9 Li, Yiyun, *Dear Friend, From My Life I Write to You in Your Life* (London 2018).

10 Keuls, Eva C., *Plato and Greek Painting* (Leiden 1978).

11 Itten, Johannes, *The Elements of Color* (New York 1970).

12 Cennini, Cennino *The Craftsman's Handbook* (New York 1954).

13 Bishop, Elizabeth, 'Arrival at Santos' in *Questions of Travel* (New York 1965).

14 Hoban, Russell, *Riddley Walker* (London 1980).

15 Yeats, W.B., 'The Circus Animals' Desertion' in *The Complete Poems* (London 1990).

16 Rich, Adrienne, 'Power' in *The Dream of a Common Language* (New York 1978).

17 Berryman, John, 'Dream Song 14' in *77 Dream Songs* (New York 1964).

18 Heaney, Seamus, 'North' in *North* (London 1975).

19 Rich, Adrienne, 'Poem XVII' from 'Twenty-One Love Poems' in *The Dream of a Common Language* (New York 1993).

20 Hoban, *Riddley Walker*.

21 Belton, Neil, *A Game with Sharpened Knives* (London 2005).

22 Kaminsky, Ilya, *Deaf Republic* (Minneapolis 2019).

23 Ferry, David, 'That Now Are Wild and Do Not Remember' in *Bewilderment* (Chicago 2012).

24 Ugrešić, Dubravka, *Thank You for Not Reading* (Dublin 2004).

25 Ugrešić, p. 203–4.

26 Constant, Caroline, *Eileen Gray* (London 2000).

27 McKim, Musa, *Night Studio: A Memoir of Philip Guston* (New York 1988).

28 Babel, Isaac, 'The Story of My Dovecot', in *Collected Stories* (London 1961).

29 Tarkovsky, Andrei, *Time Within Time: The Diaries 1970–1986*, trans. Kitty Hunter-Blair (London 1994).

30 Byrne, Martin, www.carrowkeel.com.